Morgan Charmley
Teen Witch

SCHOLASTIC

Scholastic Children's Books
An imprint of Scholastic Ltd
Euston House, 24 Eversholt Street
London, NW1 1DB, UK
Registered office: Westfield Road, Southam, Warwickshire, CV47 0RA
SCHOLASTIC and associated logos are trademarks and/or registered
trademarks of Scholastic Inc.

First published in the UK by Scholastic Ltd, 2019

Front cover character art by Nuno Ramalhão © Scholastic, 2019

ISBN 978 1407 19649 7

The right of Katy Birchall to be identified as the author
of this work has been asserted by her.

A CIP catalogue record for this work
is available from the British Library.

Printed in the UK by CPI Group (UK) Ltd, Croydon, CR0 4YY
Papers used by Scholastic Children's Books are made from wood
grown in sustainable forests.

1 3 5 7 9 10 8 6 4 2

This is a work of fiction. Names, characters, places, incidents and dialogues
are products of the author's imagination or are used fictitiously.
Any resemblance to actual people, living or dead, events or
locales is entirely coincidental.

www.scholastic.co.uk

For Ben

Chapter One

This is it. The moment I have been waiting for my entire life.

As I kneel before her, the Great Sorceress stands and lifts her arms, the long black sleeves of her cloak billowing in the wind. The crackling fire behind me is the only sound breaking through the eerie silence of the forest at night and, as the Great Sorceress takes a step towards me, the circle of witches surrounding us lift their faces to watch her expectantly.

"Morgan Charmley."

My hands are shaking and my heart thuds loudly against my chest as she intones my name. There's no going back now. I lift my eyes to meet hers.

"Morgan Charmley," she repeats, "the council has

made a decision. And I declare that . . ."

She hesitates. The other witches glance at one another in confusion. My breath catches in my throat. Why is she stopping?

No. This can't be happening. It can't be over. Not like this.

"I declare that . . ."

She pauses again. The silence is unbearable.

"Oh darling," she sighs, her voice instantly changing to a softer tone, "you've got a smudge on your face! Must be ash from the fire, come here."

She licks her thumb and reaches forward to rub my cheek.

"Mum!" I hiss, batting her hand away as the other witches start giggling. "Get off! What are you doing?"

"There, it's all gone now." She smiles with satisfaction. "Right, now, where was I?"

"You were about to do the declaration," Dora prompts cheerily. "And don't let it drag on, Aggie, my back is aching from sitting on the ground."

"Yeah," Sephy pipes up. "My bum has gone numb."

"We could just use our magic to get nice comfortable chairs. We are witches after all." Dora smiles. "Something like this, perhaps."

She clicks her fingers and is suddenly reclining

on a sofa.

"That's better," she says. "Do carry on, Aggie."

"Dora, that's not allowed." Mum laughs. "We have to go by tradition. And tradition has it that we sit in a circle on the *ground* for the results of the Young Witch Exam. You know the rules."

Mum clicks her fingers and the sofa disappears, leaving Dora sitting cross-legged on the ground again.

"I would like to have a word with the witches who decided on that tradition," Dora huffs, stubbornly crossing her arms and accidentally hitting herself in the face with her excessively large sleeve. "And I wouldn't mind asking them why we have to wear these traditional cloaks when judging the exams, too! Completely impractical."

"Ask away," Sephy says with a grin, gesturing to the witch next to her. "Mother here was one of them."

Her mother lifts her head in confusion. "What? What was that?"

"I was just saying to Dora that you helped decide on the tradition of sitting on the ground, didn't you, Mother?" Sephy shouts. "You remember? About two hundred years ago?"

"Is this stupid thing over yet?" Sephy's elderly mother replies, ignoring her. "I think it's about to rain."

Sephy sighs. "You *always* say that, Mother."

"Well, it always does." Her mother sniffs indignantly.

"Ah yes," a younger witch says from the other side of the circle. "I think I just felt a drop of rain on my nose."

The two witches either side of her murmur in agreement.

"HELLO!" I yell, waving my arms around and causing everyone to turn and look at me as though they'd forgotten I was there. "We were in the middle of something? Is there ANY chance we can take this a *little* bit seriously?"

"Sorry, Morgan," Mum says, shooting Dora and Sephy a stern look. "You're right. This is a very important moment. Now, I was just about to make the declaration, wasn't I."

She clears her throat loudly and puts on her serious voice again.

"Morgan Charmley, the council has made a decision. I declare that—"

"WAIT!" Sephy gasps, making us all jump. She holds her hands up dramatically, closes her eyes and inhales deeply.

"*What*, Sephy?" Mum asks, looking baffled as we all stare at Sephy in anticipation. "What's wrong?"

She eventually opens her eyes. "Yep. It is *definitely* raining."

I bury my head in my hands with a groan, as the

witches begin to grumble about the English weather. Umbrellas appear out of thin air, shielding everyone in the circle. Mum clicks her fingers at the fire and winks at me. "Those flames are now waterproof."

"Great," I mutter under my breath. "Any chance you can throw me into them?"

"Oh, I wouldn't recommend that, Morgan," Dora chips in. The umbrella over her head is in the shape of a bright-pink, glittery flamingo. "It takes ages to get the soot out of your hair."

The witches around me launch into various discussions about the weather and haircare tips, while I sit back on my feet and sigh heavily. I start thinking the worst. Maybe they're putting off giving me my results on purpose. Maybe I failed and they don't want to tell me the bad news.

Again.

You'd think they'd be well-practised at it considering this is my eighth time taking the Young Witch Exam, or YWE. I was five years old when I first had a crack at it and it went fairly badly. And by fairly, I mean colossally. Dora instructed me to make a turnip float in the air for three seconds and lower it gently again.

It was a standard YWE task. I'd practised it loads of times at home. I tried to focus on the turnip and not be so nervous. I tried to swallow the lump in my throat and ignore how dry my mouth was. I tried to stop my hand from shaking as I clicked my fingers and . . .

. . . I turned Dora into a turnip. It was deeply traumatizing for the both of us.

She was very nice about it and Mum reversed the spell straight away, so it wasn't like she was a turnip for very long or anything. Dora kept going on about how it showed that I had great powers, being able to turn a person into a turnip at the age of five, but I soon proved her wrong. The following year I failed again, and then the year after that, and the year after that, and so on.

I have no idea if I've passed this time round. I didn't turn anyone into a turnip during today's exam, which is promising, but when Dora stepped forward and instructed me to produce "a basket of pears wearing mini top hats" I hesitated, giving her a strange look, and I know they deduct points for hesitation.

But what kind of exam question is that?! When in my life am I ever going to need to suddenly have a basket of pears with top hats? I noticed Mum rolling her eyes at Dora's request, but she didn't make her change the task.

Dora looked pleased with the pears I produced, so hopefully my hesitation hasn't affected my result too much. She picked one up from the wicker basket I was suddenly holding to examine it and burst out laughing, holding it up to the rest of the circle and going, "Look at this pear! It has a top hat on! A pear with a top hat! HA!"

She also asked me to make a large branch on the ground float through the air and move around a bit before landing gently, which I did perfectly, but I am slightly worried that I took too long on the third task – fix a broken shower that appeared in front of me out of thin air. I managed to fix it, but not before two of the witches got drenched by the out-of-control showerhead that was flying all over the place. They both gave Dora, who was trying not to laugh, very sour looks as they clicked their fingers and were magicked dry again.

I just really, really, REALLY hope I did well enough to finally pass.

The YWE is the most important exam you can take as a witch, because it means that you are good enough at spells and controlling your magical powers to be permitted to go to school. It means that you're trusted not to expose the secret that witches still exist and always have. And one of the best things about passing the YWE is that you're allowed to take broomstick-flying lessons.

I've never passed it, so I've never been allowed to go to school or learn how to fly. Instead, I've been home-schooled all my life. Not that it's been too bad or anything. Dora, my mum's best friend and our next-door neighbour, is my tutor and she is a lot of fun to be around, being completely bonkers.

But still, I've had to sit at home with my books all day every day, knowing that other witches my age get to go to school and make friends.

Dora's great but the other day she referred to her phone as her "portable communicator machine". And she finds pieces of fruit wearing top hats hilarious. It would be *really* nice to hang out with people my age for a change.

I guess I haven't exactly helped my case over the years – there have been a couple of completely innocent magical mishaps. Mum has never forgiven me for the time I turned that stupid boy into a toad, even though he deserved it. A few years ago, I was in the park with Mum and Dora, trying out my new bike. As I put on my helmet, this boy went past on his skateboard and yelled out, "HA HA, PEA-HEAD!"

Look, I stick to my story: I angrily clenched my hands and just HAPPENED to click my fingers accidentally.

Next thing I knew, there was a toad riding a skateboard.

I thought it was pretty funny and had anyone been

around to film a toad riding a skateboard, I'm certain it would have been a YouTube sensation, but Mum went ballistic about the whole incident. She turned him back to his stupid self but she couldn't erase his memory, because only potions can do that. And witches don't do potions. Warlocks do.

Witches hate warlocks and the feeling is mutual.

Mum was really angry about having to go to the Chief Warlock and ask him for help to sort out my mess. There's nothing more humiliating for a witch than having to ask a warlock for help. I was grounded FOR EVER and lectured for weeks.

"You can't go around turning people into toads!" Mum kept saying.

"I will if they call me a pea-head!" I argued.

"That's not how being a witch works!" Mum said, exasperated. "You can't do that sort of thing in the real world."

"If I can't turn a boy into a toad when he calls me a pea-head, then WHAT is the point of being a witch?" I yelled back.

She didn't have an answer for that one, and even though NOW, a few years on, I can understand why I shouldn't have lost my temper and turned him into a toad, I also stand by the fact that he deserved it and was a much nicer toad than boy.

But, whatever.

The point is that I am turning thirteen in a few days and I am a VERY mature and VERY capable witch, ready to go to normal school and make normal friends without giving the game away that I have magical powers. I should have passed the exam YEARS ago, but I kept mucking up. It's like I couldn't handle the pressure or something, and even though I KNEW that I was able to pass the exam, I just kept failing it.

Which, by the way, isn't exactly great when you're the daughter of the Great Sorceress. It kind of makes failing the exam ten billion times worse.

"Don't be silly, Morgan," Mum said last year after I'd failed again. "That has nothing to do with anything."

"Mum," I sighed, "you're the Great Sorceress. You are so good at magic that you were nominated by all the witches in Britain to be in charge of the Witch Council and make all the important witch decisions."

"The youngest ever candidate to be voted in as the Great Sorceress," Mum said with a dreamy look on her face, before checking herself at my frown. "Not that that's important. It's only a silly title."

"Still. Everyone expects me to be brilliant, like you

were. Instead, I'm a complete disaster."

"No, you're not," she said sternly. "You *are* brilliant. You just don't believe you are. And during the exam, in front of the scrutinizing eyes of everyone on the Witch Council, you panic under pressure and make mistakes, just like plenty of other brilliant witches have done before you. Next year, you'll pass with flying colours."

So, here I am. Waiting to hear the results of the exam that has been hanging over my head for as long as I can remember.

And everyone is too busy talking about the rain.

"I remember the great storm of eighteen fifty-nine," Sephy's mother says in a gloomy voice. "You should have seen those winds. Nothing like it."

"Oh yes, I remember." Another elderly witch across the circle nods. "Almost blew my chimney right off."

"MUM!" I cry loudly above the noise. "Did I fail? Please, just put me out of my misery. It's OK, I can take it."

The circle falls silent. Mum takes a deep breath.

"No, Morgan Charmley," she says gently, a smile creeping across her lips. "You did it. You passed."

Chapter Two

The forest erupts with loud cheers and cries of congratulations from the Witch Council as I hop up and down on the spot screaming, "YES! FINALLY!"

"Well done, Morgan," Mum laughs, stepping forward and putting her hands on my shoulders so I face her straight on. She looks me in the eye. "You did very well. I'm proud of you."

"Congratulations, Morgan," Dora says, standing up with a loud creak and enveloping me in a huge hug.

As I pull away, I look up to see enormous tears rolling down Dora's face.

"Dora! Why are you crying?" I say. "This is the BEST NEWS EVER! You can go back to having a life! You don't have to tutor me any more!"

Dora's expression crumples and she bursts into loud, heaving sobs. I look to Mum, baffled, but she just smiles warmly and puts an arm around her best friend's shoulders.

"It would appear that your tutor has grown rather fond of her pupil."

"Nonsense," Dora says sternly, blowing her nose with a blue polka-dot handkerchief. "I'm thrilled about this situation. I'll have plenty of free time on my hands to take up some interesting hobbies and you ... well, you ... will go off ... to school ... all grown-up..."

Unable to continue, Dora flings her arms out and pulls me towards her again, holding me so tight that I find it tricky to breathe.

"I'll still see you all the time, Dora, you live next door," I point out, my voice muffled in her shoulder. "And it's probably a good thing for me to finally make some new friends and do things on my own."

"You're never on your own," a dry, bored voice says from my feet. "Due to a dismal stroke of luck, we're stuck to each other for ever more."

Merlin. I'd almost forgotten he was there.

Despite the magic side of things, there is one huge disadvantage of being a witch: you have to have a "familiar".

That's what gave us witches away a lot back in the sixteenth century, when everyone lost their heads and began to hunt us down. Every witch has a familiar, a spirit guide, and back then any mysterious woman with a black cat was a suspect.

I wish I could have a nice, fluffy, normal pet cat instead of a familiar. Sadly, like most aspects of my life, my familiar is a DISASTER. Yeah, don't be fooled by the idea of an adorable sidekick guiding you through life, together through everything, an unconditional bond. Merlin spends the majority of his time pointing out my flaws and making jokes about them. Like the other day, when he asked me if I'd noticed the fact I have quite hairy hands for a girl.

I hadn't noticed that before. Now it's all I can think about.

Merlin, like all witch familiars, is a shape-shifter. They can't become human, but they can become pretty much anything else. And they're with you for ever. Which means that Merlin will never leave my side. For my whole life.

It's all very depressing.

For this year's YWE, he decided to take the form of a wasp so he could annoy all the witches by buzzing around their ears, until Mum gave him a VERY stern look and he quickly transformed himself into a rat and settled down by the fire.

My mum can be very intimidating when she wants to be, being the Great Sorceress and everything.

"Merlin," I sigh, "I know that you're happy for me, whatever you say. Now that I've passed my exam, life will be a bit more interesting, don't you think?"

"Life is overrated," he says with a yawn, receiving a glare from Mum's familiar, Helena, who is standing next to Mum in the form of a Bengal cat.

"You could show Morgan a little more support," Helena hisses at him. "She's worked hard for this goal and as her familiar you should be pleased that she's achieved such—"

"Blah blah blah," Merlin interrupts rudely. "Is this thing over yet?"

"Honestly!" Helena says, her fur bristling. "I don't know how you put up with him, Morgan!"

"It's a daily struggle," I admit.

"And to think," Merlin says, ignoring us, "I could be in Bora Bora right now with that nice witch, Lydia Cooper. She was really something."

I roll my eyes at Mum. Merlin likes to constantly remind me that he was considered for the role of familiar for Lydia Cooper, a young witch who lives in Bora Bora.

Sadly (in his opinion), he was assigned to me instead and doomed to a life of misery.

"Stop it, Merlin," Mum says. "We all know that's not true. Every familiar has a chosen witch by destiny; you wouldn't be considered for anyone else."

"I bet Lydia Cooper is drinking coconut water right now, looking out at the deep turquoise sea," Merlin sighs. "I, on the other hand, am in a forest in the middle of Essex with some witches dancing around a fire in the rain and a very confused-looking man with terrible fashion sense."

"What?" Mum asks, looking startled. "What do you mean, a man with—"

She gasps, following Merlin's gaze.

"Dora!" she cries, grabbing her best friend's arm and pointing over my shoulder.

Dora's husband is standing in the forest wearing a warm fleece and head torch, with a camera round his neck, staring at us in horror.

Dora spins round and lets out a long sigh. "Oh, not again."

"D-Dora?" he stammers, his eyes wide as saucers as all the witches stop dancing round the fire. "W-what are y-you—"

"Hello, Howard!" Dora waves cheerily. "Out for a spot of badger-watching, are you? You should have told me!"

She turns to Mum. "Don't worry, Aggie, I have some of that warlock's memory potion left over from the last time this happened. I'll make sure he drinks it this evening and it will all be a distant dream in no time. I'll see you back at home."

"Thank you, Dora." Mum smiles. "And hello, Howard, nice to see you!"

Dora leads him away as he continues to splutter in shock and Mum turns to the rest of the group.

"Well, I think that's all for tonight. Lovely to see you and I look forward to the next meeting."

We wave goodbye to the witches and they disappear into the night, crying out congratulations to me as they leave on their broomsticks. Mum puts a hand on my shoulder and squeezes it, lowering the hood of her cloak.

"You did it, Morgan. I knew you would." She grins proudly.

"Took me long enough."

"Don't we know it," Merlin mutters, but I don't even care because NOTHING can ruin how happy I am feeling in this moment, not even my grouchy familiar.

"It doesn't matter," Mum says, shooting a sharp look at Merlin. "You got there. Are you ready for your next adventure?"

I click my fingers and send a burst of fireworks shooting up, exploding into a rainbow of colours across the night sky. Merlin, who has now transformed himself into a small monkey perched on my shoulder, covers his ears grumpily.

"Yes." I grin. "I'm ready."

Chapter Three

A few days after my exam, I wake up to loud whispers outside my door.

"Come on! Quick! Before she wakes up!"

"I'm coming!"

"Careful of that squeaky floorboard!"

"Which one?"

"The one just there."

"Which one just where?"

"You know! That one, right there!"

"Oh yes, of course, I'll step round it."

There is a loud creaking noise as a foot presses down on the squeaky floorboard at the top of the stairs. I smile to myself at the deathly silence that immediately follows, before the whispers start again.

"You HAD to step on the ONE floorboard that squeaks."

"You were pointing at a different floorboard!"

"My finger was practically touching it!"

"No, it wasn't! It was pointing to the right! Honestly, you'd think you'd know your own floorboards."

Merlin, who has been nestled on my pillow as a dormouse all night, transforms into a spiky hedgehog.

"Can they just get on with it?" he spits, curling into a ball.

"Shh!" I frown, closing my eyes and pretending to be asleep.

"OK," I hear my mum whisper. "Shall we go in now?"

"Yes, let's do it."

"On the count of three. And yell 'Surprise' loudly."

"'Surprise'? Really? Shouldn't we yell 'Happy Birthday'?"

"But it's a big surprise."

"But it's also her birthday."

"FINE. We'll yell 'Happy Birthday'."

"Hmm. Maybe 'Surprise' is better. Snappier."

"*DORA!*"

"I'm ready! Let's go in!"

"One ... two ... three!"

The door bursts open, lights come on and at a click

of my mum's fingers, dozens of colourful streamers burst through the air of my bedroom, glitter cascades from the ceiling and a huge purple-iced cake comes floating towards me.

"HAPPY BIRTHDAY!" cries Mum.

"SURPRISE!" yells Dora at the same time.

They look at each other in confusion and I burst out laughing, while Merlin burrows under the pillow grumpily. He's never been much of a morning person.

"This is amazing." I smile, watching the glitter float down all around me, handily disappearing before it reaches the floor so there's no mess. Such a typical Mum spell. "Thank you!"

"Happy thirteenth birthday, Morgan." Mum comes over to pull me into a hug. "What an exciting year ahead!"

"I can't believe you're a teenager," Dora says, her eyes watering as she steps round my bed to plant a big kiss on my cheek. "I remember the day you were born."

"Time flies," Helena says fondly. She's in the form of a butterfly, fluttering around the cake that is still hovering in the air.

"Don't encourage Dora, Helena," chuckles Mac, Dora's familiar, who is in his favourite form: a corgi. "The waterworks are about to start."

"Oh hush, you," Dora says, patting his head. "I just have glitter in my eye."

"Let's go downstairs and get breakfast ready, shall we?" Mum laughs, winking at me and guiding Dora from the room as she dabs at her eyes with her sleeves. "We'll see you down there, Birthday Girl."

I'm so excited for the day that it doesn't take me long to get ready. When I've finished getting dressed and tying up my hair, I skip downstairs and head into the kitchen, Merlin reluctantly following in the form of a black cat.

Mum and Dora are sitting at the kitchen table, Mum sipping from a mug of coffee, her second of the day no doubt, and Dora with a large pot of tea in front of her. When they're next to each other, their differences are so stark, it would be surprising to a stranger to learn that they are the best of friends. Mum is sensible, authoritative and calm. Dora is spontaneous, loud and disorganized. Their clothes are completely at odds: in normal life, Mum is a CEO of an advertising company so she's always dressed smartly. Today she's wearing a white high-neck blouse with black culottes, while Dora is in one of her signature multi-coloured outfits: a neon-pink flowery top and a lime-green skirt.

You can't help but smile when Dora walks into a room. She's always a burst of colour.

Mum and Dora have been best friends for years and when Mum fell pregnant with me, she decided to move into the house next door to Dora, who by then had married Howard – who doesn't know she's a witch – and moved to Essex. Mum doesn't like talking about my dad and all I know about him is that he walked out, which is why she moved to be near Dora. I have no idea if he ever knew that Mum was a witch and I don't like to ask questions about him, because even though Mum pretends she's fine, her face always crumples slightly when he's mentioned. I never feel like I'm missing out by not having him around though, because I kind of have two mums. Dora has been there for as long as I can remember.

Sometimes when I'm mad at Mum, I storm out and walk the five paces it takes to go to Dora's house. She's great at cheering me up and if she doesn't manage it, then Howard will. He is HILARIOUS. I've never met anyone who is as enthusiastic as Howard is – about absolutely everything. He's a teacher too, but not a tutor like Dora. He teaches science at a local school. They're both crazy about animals and foster loads at a time. At the moment, they have twelve dogs, five cats, three pigs, one ferret, several hamsters and a python in their house.

Howard also thinks that they own a corgi called Mac.

Mum's and Dora's familiars get on as well as they do: Helena loves to remark on the fact that Mac appears to be always sleeping, while Mac enjoys teasing her about how prim and proper she is.

Neither of them like Merlin.

Which I can totally relate to.

"There she is." Mum beams, beckoning me to join them at the table. "What would you like for breakfast? Pancakes?"

I nod excitedly and Mum clicks her fingers, producing a plate stacked with pancakes dripping in treacle in front of me. As I dig in, I glance up at the clock on the wall.

"Mum," I say through a mouthful, "you're going to be late for work."

"I know, I'd better get going," she sighs, getting up and grabbing her smart handbag from the side counter. "Are you sure you don't mind me working today? I promise we'll celebrate properly this evening when we do presents."

"Dora is going to take me into town," I say happily, as Mum kisses me goodbye. "We're going birthday shopping."

"Oh yes," Dora says, her eyes twinkling. "I know just the place to go."

*

"*Here?*"

I cross my arms, looking up at the shop that Dora has brought me to.

"Dora," I groan, "I don't want to go into another pet shop! We've already been to two this morning."

"Yes, but this one stocks the new FERRET WHEEL!" She laughs. "Get it? Like Ferris wheel! But for ferrets!"

I don't react.

She clears her throat. "Anyway, I'm desperate to get one and I know they sell them in here."

"Why don't you just click your fingers and magic one up?"

She gives me a disapproving look. "Keep that voice down, Morgan. And in answer to your question, sometimes it's fun to browse and then pick out something and buy it, rather than just get everything you want in a matter of seconds."

I glance around me to try to find a better option and notice a shop standing on its own down a deserted alleyway nearby, away from the buzz of the high street. There's a rickety old sign with chipped paint hanging above the door announcing this shop as *Blaze Books: Second-hand and Antique Books.*

Dora once told me that in some old bookshops in

Essex, you can still find sorcery books and memoirs written centuries ago by witches. She is always going on about how we live in a county full of witchcraft history. When witches were hunted back in the sixteenth century, Essex was pretty much the centre of the hysteria – loads of our kind got "killed" here. Their acting was second to none.

All of them live to tell the tale.

Anyway, apparently most of these old memoirs detail all the evil curses the witches put on people back then. After the witch trials, they were VERY bitter and recorded their acts of revenge. Dora said I should avoid those books at all costs. According to her, they are grim.

I think they sound AWESOME. I'm yet to find one, but I love going into old bookshops just in case.

"You go into the pet shop, Dora, and get your ferret wheel. I'm going to have a wander and then I'll find you when you're done," I suggest.

"You're not going for a wander on your own," she says. "All right, we don't have to go into the pet shop. Where do you want to go?"

I point to the bookshop down the alleyway and she frowns.

"No, we're not going there."

"Why not?"

She hesitates. "Because it's a rubbish bookshop. Terrible stock. Tried to find a Christmas present for Howard in there once and it was useless! Come on, how about we go to a department store and have a look round the clothes? You can pick something out for your birthday."

Dora loves bookshops. She's a TUTOR. Which means there can only be one reason she doesn't want to go into *that* specific bookshop: she knows that those old, horrible witch books are in there and she doesn't want me to find one, read it and be traumatized.

Naturally, that means I *have* to go in there. An idea hits me.

"You know what, Dora, I'm being stupid – let's go into the pet shop."

Her face brightens. "Really?"

"Yeah! I really want to see all the . . . pet food and stuff."

"Great! You're going to love it in here, Morgan." She claps her hands together as I walk enthusiastically alongside her into the shop. "They have a whole section of toys for chinchillas!"

"Cool! How about I go find the chilliechin section and you get the ferret wheel."

"*Chinchillas*, silly," she corrects cheerfully, before

hurrying off down an aisle. "Chinchilla accessories are at the back. I'll meet you there. See you in a second!"

As soon as she disappears around the corner, I dart out of the shop and down the alley towards the bookshop.

"You escaped from a lame pet shop, so that you could go to a boring second-hand bookshop," sighs Merlin, in the form of a beetle on my shoulder. "Wow. I really am stuck with the dorkiest teenage witch in history."

I ignore him, pushing open the door to the shop. A large old bell rings above my head and a tall man with dark, messy hair appears from behind a stack of books at the counter.

"Hello there!" he says chirpily, sliding the books along so he can lean forward. "Welcome to Blaze Books. Are you looking for anything in particular?"

I shake my head. "Just having a look around."

"Enjoy." He smiles, gesturing to the shelves before returning his attention to the pile of books in front of him.

I head towards the history section at the back, guessing that the oldest books may be lurking around there somewhere. The shop is completely empty and silent. It's so peaceful in here compared to the high street.

"Why don't you just ask that man where the sorcery books are?" Merlin says in a tired voice.

"Oh yeah, because that wouldn't be weird," I reply sarcastically, my eyes scanning the rows in front of me. "Merlin, I can't just stroll up to someone and say, 'Excuse me but do you happen to have some old sorcery books lying around?'."

"Actually, we *do* have some sorcery books."

I yelp at the hidden voice and whack my head against the bookshelf behind me.

"Ouch! Are you OK?" A boy emerges from behind the row I was peering at.

"I'm fine thank you," I say hurriedly, rubbing the back of my head and ignoring Merlin's sniggers as he tucks himself under the collar of my T-shirt. "You made me jump."

"Sorry." The boy grins. "I thought you'd seen me. Who were you talking to?"

"When?"

"Just now. About the sorcery books."

"Myself," I say. "I . . . I was talking out loud."

He nods slowly. "I do that too when I think no one's watching. I'm Owen Blaze, by the way. You probably met my dad at the counter when you came in."

I think Owen is about my age. He's taller than me

with very dark, scruffy hair that looks like it hasn't been brushed in forever, dark eyes and a small birthmark on his cheek.

"I'm Morgan." I glance around the shelves. "Are there really sorcery books in here?"

"Yeah, folktale spells and stuff," he says, putting on a spooky voice. "You interested in that kind of thing?"

"No, no, don't be stupid," I reply quickly, shaking my head.

I don't have much experience of making friends, but I'm going to take a wild guess that being into ancient sorcery books and folktales doesn't make a brilliant first impression.

"Obviously books like that are full of rubbish," I add casually, just to emphasize my point.

"Obviously," he says, watching me curiously. "Kind of cool, though. I can try to find one for you, if you'd like."

"It's OK, it was just a stupid thought."

I pretend to browse the row of books in front of me, annoyed that he's still lingering. If he goes away, then maybe I'll have a chance of finding the books he's talking about on my own. My phone begins ringing loudly in my bag. I jump at the sudden noise and thump the back of my head against the bookshelf again.

"You should really stop banging your head," Owen suggests, wincing.

"Thanks for the advice," I mutter, reaching into my bag for my phone. Dora's name is flashing on the screen and as soon as the call rings out, she rings again.

"I have to go," I tell Owen, gesturing to my phone.

"See you around."

He disappears into another aisle as I pick up and Dora immediately launches into a huge lecture about how I shouldn't have left the shop and how worried she's been.

"I'm coming, Dora," I say quickly, heading towards the door and giving Owen's dad a grateful nod. He waves cheerily. "I was just in a clothes shop. Yeah, I didn't want to disturb you and thought I'd have a look at some jeans and—"

I stop talking as soon as I leave the shop, lowering my phone. Dora is standing outside, her jaw clenched and her eyes narrowed to slits. She does not look happy.

"Busted," Merlin cackles.

Seriously, how come I got stuck with the familiar who takes pleasure in my mishaps?! Why couldn't I have got a guide who, oh I don't know, ACTUALLY GUIDES ME?

"Do you know how terrified I was when I couldn't

find you? I practically tore the chinchilla section apart looking for you!" Dora cries, as Merlin tucks himself away under my collar to have a snooze.

"Sorry, Dora, really I am. I didn't mean to worry you," I say gently, watching her expression immediately soften. She can never stay angry at me for long.

"Well?" Her eyes flicker nervously towards the door of Blaze Books. "Was it worth it?"

"No," I say, linking my arm through hers. "There was nothing interesting in there."

"Told you." She smiles in relief before leading me back towards the high street. "There are much better bookshops elsewhere."

As we walk away, I look over my shoulder at the bookshop. A curtain twitches in the upstairs window and, even though there's no one there, the whole way down the street I can't shake the feeling that I'm being watched.

Chapter Four

"All right!" Dora exclaims, making the huge birthday cake decorated with thirteen candles float just in front of me. "Make a curse!"

"Dora, really," Mum sighs. "That old witch tradition died out years ago."

"I like to keep it alive." Dora grins, her eyes twinkling with mischief. "What better way to celebrate a birthday than to curse someone who has been irritating you? I don't know why making a curse as you blow out your candles ever went out of fashion! What's the point in witches making a wish? We can just magic whatever we want."

"Can I curse Merlin even though he's my familiar?" I ask.

"Careful, young witch," Merlin snarls. He's in the form of a skunk and lifts his tail threateningly. "You want to start your school career stinking so bad no one comes near you?"

"Unfortunately, if you were to curse Merlin, you would also automatically curse yourself," Dora tells me apologetically.

"You can't curse *anyone* by blowing out a few birthday candles." Mum laughs, shaking her head at us. "It's a load of nonsense, as you both well know. And if you don't blow those candles out soon, they'll be going out on their own."

"Spoilsport," Dora whispers to Mum before turning to me excitedly. "Make a curse anyway, Morgan. It's bad luck if you don't."

Mum lifts her eyes to the ceiling and mutters something about "old witch tales". I shut my eyes and, taking a deep breath, blow out all the candles in one go. They both cheer loudly and Mum gives me a hug before clicking her fingers. The cake slices itself and three pieces appear on plates that come to land in front of each of us.

"Well? Who did you curse?" Dora asks eagerly, lifting her fork.

"If I told you, it wouldn't come true."

"Of course, of course," she says, nodding. "You're quite right."

But the truth is, I didn't make a curse. And that's because I don't really know that many people yet and I like everyone I do know. Being home-schooled all my life, I haven't exactly had the chance to spend time with anyone I might want to curse.

I guess, if I really wanted to, I could curse that arrogant guy across the road who made fun of my outfit one time – it had been VERY early in the morning and I was VERY tired and in a moment of EXHAUSTION forgot that I had already put jeans on when I pulled a dress over my head – but Mum took care of that one.

She gave him this *really* hard stare and told him that she thought it was cool that I was expressing my individuality and not conforming to the social norm of wearing jeans OR a dress. She said he should respect that.

Mum refused to let me go and change on principle and then ushered me down the road, instructing me to keep my chin up and "own the look". I don't know if I succeeded in doing that, but what I *do* know is that Mum clicked her fingers with a sly smile on her face as we walked off and for two weeks after that, everywhere that guy went, people pointed and laughed at his outfit.

According to Mum, he hasn't made fun of what anyone chooses to wear since.

"Is it present time now?" Dora asks, clapping her hands so loudly she scares the life out of Mac, who has been fast asleep at her feet in corgi form. He jumps up and starts barking at nothing.

Merlin sniggers at him. "Disturbing your beauty sleep, were we, Mac? God knows you need it."

Merlin transforms into a hyena and begins screeching with laughter at his own joke, rolling on his back on the kitchen floor. Everyone gives him an unimpressed look and I bury my head in my hands. Mac sighs, transforms into a monkey and jumps up on to Dora's shoulder, wrapping his tail around her neck.

"Do I have permission to put Merlin in his place, Dora?"

"I'm afraid not," Dora says. "It's Morgan's birthday dinner. Any other time and I might have allowed it."

"Please don't hold back on my behalf," I say cheerily.

Merlin stops cackling, narrows his eyes at me and then transforms into a large brown bear and sits on my lap, squashing me with his weight.

"GERROFF!" I yell, my voice muffled in his stinky fur.

"Not until you say sorry," he huffs.

"YOU'RE SQUISHING ME!"

"Say. Sorry," he repeats, wriggling his bum.

"FINE! SORRY!"

He transforms into a black cat and curls up into a ball in my lap, looking up at me with huge green innocent eyes. I scowl at him and then notice that Mum and Dora are trying and failing to suppress giggles.

"You know, by laughing you're only encouraging him," I remark grumpily, before absent-mindedly stroking his ears.

"Where were we?" Helena asks. She's perched on the table in the form of a Bengal cat, elegantly licking her paw and showing no interest in Merlin's antics whatsoever. "Wasn't it present time?"

"Yes, thank you, Helena." Mum smiles. "Dora, would you like to go first?"

"YES!" Dora pulls a terribly-wrapped present out of her bag and slides it along the table towards me. "I'm so glad you passed your YWE, Morgan, because I think this will be very helpful at school."

"Thanks, Dora." I beam at her before ripping the paper excitedly. I hesitate as I see what it is. "Wow. It's ... um..."

"Do you like it?"

It's a very large backpack covered in broomsticks, black cats and witch hats.

"Isn't that amazing?" she says, and Mum nods in agreement. "I found it in this little boutique shop in that town, Manningtree. I couldn't believe how perfect it was. You can put all your school books in there, Morgan!"

"Wow, thanks! It's great!" I say, with as much enthusiasm as I can muster. "Are you sure this won't give away that I'm a witch, though? Maybe I shouldn't bring it to school just in case."

Dora shakes her head, chuckling. "But that's the whole JOKE! Everyone is going to say, 'Oh look, there's Morgan with her cool witch backpack' when in fact you're an ACTUAL WITCH!"

"Ha ha ha, yeah, that's hilarious," I say with a fixed smile. "I guess. Thanks, Dora!"

"She might as well put a sign on your back saying 'please make fun of me'," Merlin mutters, but Mum and Dora are laughing too loudly to hear.

"Now," Mum says, once they've finished admiring the backpack, "it's my turn."

She clicks her fingers and a thin, flat, beautifully-wrapped box floats out of a drawer and lands neatly in front of me.

"Thanks, Mum," I say, untying the bow.

Once I've ripped open the paper, I lift the lid of the box and gasp, looking down at a stunning necklace with a delicate gold chain. The pendant is a striking deep-sea blue and, as I look closer, I can see that the colour is gently swirling. I blink up at Mum in amazement.

"Do you like it?" she asks anxiously. "My mum gave it to me when I turned sixteen. I was thinking of waiting until then to give it to you, but you've worked so hard to pass your YWE exam and, well . . . now seemed like the right time."

"Mum," I say quietly, lifting it from its box. "I love it. It's beautiful."

"Put it on," Helena prompts, her bright cat eyes glistening with tears.

"Let me help," Mum says. She takes it carefully and places it around my neck, standing behind me to close the clasp. "There. It suits you."

"Oh, Morgan," Dora croaks as Mac, still in his monkey form, pats her comfortingly on the shoulder.

"What a very touching moment," Merlin sneers. "Someone pass me the tissues, will ya?"

"What is this stone?" I ask Mum, ignoring him. "It's so unusual."

"I don't think it's particularly expensive or anything," she says breezily, clicking her fingers to put the kettle on. "But it is priceless to our family. I believe your great grandmother was given it by a warlock who was desperately in love with her, and it's been passed down since then."

"My great grandmother was in love with a warlock?"

Mum looks horrified at the idea. "No! Of course not. Witches could never associate with warlocks. But it's no surprise that a warlock might fall in love with a witch. We are their superiors in every way."

"So, she didn't love him but she took the necklace anyway?" I examine the pendant. "That doesn't sound right. Maybe she was secretly in love with him too."

"No chance." Dora snorts. "Warlocks are impossible. What qualities would you fall in love with? The fact that they have no sense of humour? Their lack of manners or compassion? And all those insults they constantly throw?"

"Ugh, don't get me started on warlocks," Mum says, sitting back down at the table in time for a cup of tea to land in front of her and slide into her grasp. "Last week, one of them decided to attempt an entirely new potion recipe that apparently HAD to have water from the Thames. Thanks to camera phones, he was filmed wading into the river from the South Bank with his cauldron, and it went viral. I had to have several meetings with the Chief Warlock to remind him of his responsibilities to keep his kind under control." She shakes her head and sighs. "I *hate* having meetings with the Chief Warlock. He cannot stop spitting as he talks."

Dora wrinkles her nose. "Warlocks are the *worst* kind of folk."

That is one of the first lessons you learn as a witch. Warlocks are our greatest enemy. The undeniable truth that all warlocks are selfish, rude, power-hungry and not that great at magic is woven into witch culture. Witches are always making fun of the fact that warlocks can't just click their fingers and get what they want – they have to create a potion in a cauldron, some of which can take days to make, and then they have to drink the potion to unlock any kind of magical power.

Warlocks would LOVE to be as powerful as witches and hate that they're not, which makes them bitter, horrible people. In every storybook read to young witches, the villain is a warlock.

I used to be a little bit sceptical about the whole all-warlocks-are-evil thing because of the time I sneaked into Mum's home office where, as the Great Sorceress, she has loads of witch and warlock books. I managed to read one fairy tale from the warlock book I picked off the shelf before she caught me in there and kicked me out, taking the book from my hands and saying, "These books are filled with lies and rubbish."

But guess who was the evil villain in that story? Yeah, a witch. According to that tale, witches glow in the dark because the evil shines through our skin.

To which I can only say ... I WISH.

Just the other day, I got out of bed to go to the toilet in the middle of the night and I walked straight into my wardrobe. Glowing evil skin would have really helped me out.

Anyway, reading that story made me question whether all the bad things I'd read about warlocks were true. Maybe there were nice warlocks out there.

But then I met the warlock Daisy Hornbuckle – a common misconception in popular culture is that all warlocks are male – and any question over warlocks and whether they were actually that bad swiftly evaporated.

When I was eight years old, Mum and I had been on our way to the theatre to see a Saturday matinee performance in London. There was a big disaster and we had to turn back – a warlock had tried making a potion and accidentally melted their cauldron, so the potion spilled out everywhere and destroyed their entire building. The warlock, finding it hilarious, posted a picture of the ruined house online.

We had to go for an emergency meeting with the

Chief Warlock. Mum was so angry, she could barely talk on the way to his house and when we got there, she instructed me to wait outside his study while she, in her words, "went in there to kick some warlock butt".

I was sitting there happily minding my own business while Merlin flitted about the room in the form of a moth, when a stern-faced woman with grey hair and big round spectacles walked in.

Daisy Hornbuckle. The Chief Warlock's cousin, who was staying with him for a few days.

She saw me and stopped in her tracks.

"Hi!" I said with a cheery wave. "I'm Morgan Charmley."

Her face contorted into an ugly expression – her nose wrinkled, her eyebrows arched, her cheeks sucked in as though she had eaten a super-sour sweet.

"I KNOW WHO YOU ARE!" she bellowed, giving me such a fright that I almost peed myself right there and then. "HOW DARE YOU SIT ON THAT CHAIR? HOW DARE YOU BE IN THIS HOUSE WITH YOUR WITCH GERMS? WITCH! WITCH! GET OUT!"

She lunged at me and started chasing me around the room, screeching, "WITCH! DISGUSTING WITCH! SMELLY WITCH!" at the top of her lungs.

I have never been so petrified in my life and because

43

I was in a state of panic and fear, I instinctively clicked my fingers when she backed me into a corner.

Having heard the commotion, Mum and the Chief Warlock came bursting through the doors and found me cowering in the corner next to an ice statue of Daisy Hornbuckle. Merlin, now in the form of a woodpecker, was pecking ferociously at her frozen head.

So yeah, I can confirm that as Dora says, warlocks are absolutely, one hundred per cent, no doubt about it, the WORST.

"Anyway, I'm glad you like the necklace, Morgan," Mum says brightly, smiling at me. "And this weekend, we'll get everything you need before term starts."

"You won't need to think about getting a backpack now though," Dora says, winking at me. "You are *welcome*."

"I can't believe you're off to school." Mum chuckles, shaking her head. "You seem much too young."

"Are you kidding? I'm thirteen!" I gesture to the half-eaten cake. "It's about time I went to school."

"Yes." Dora nods, reaching over to take Mum's hand and squeeze it. "It had to happen sometime."

"I hope I make friends," I say quietly, biting my lip. "What if no one likes me?"

Since I passed the YWE, I haven't been sleeping

well due to a mixture of excitement and nerves. I can't wait to finally get the chance to go to school but I'm also terrified of not fitting in. I HAVE to make friends.

"Don't be silly, Morgan, they'll love you. Just be yourself," Dora says gently.

"Yes, although..." Mum hesitates. "Not *completely* yourself, of course."

"I know, no witch stuff allowed," I assure her.

"Right." She nods. "No magic at school. It's just too risky, if anything were to go wrong, or if anyone saw—"

"I didn't use any spells at school until I passed my Young Adult Witch Exam at sixteen," Dora chips in, referring to the next level test all witches take in their mid-teens. "By the time you pass that one, you're fully in control of your magic and unlikely to make any mistakes. It's the best way to keep our secret safe."

"I could not agree more," Mum says. "So just promise me, Morgan, that—"

"Seriously, I have been waiting to go to school my whole life. Do you *really* think I'm going to risk it all by casting a few spells? Don't worry, I won't use any magic when I'm there," I say confidently, smiling at them. "I promise."

Chapter Five

"I can't believe it," I whisper, standing at the school gates. "I'm finally here."

Mum puts her hand on my shoulder. In front of the main school building there are clusters of students hanging out on the steps; others are kicking around a football; some are standing in groups, clutching books to their chest and laughing together. It looks EXACTLY like a normal school scene from a film. And I get to step into it after having waited so, so long.

"This is it," I say, smiling up at Mum. "I'll see you later."

"Good luck, Morgan," she says, pretending not to be blinking back tears. "Dora will pick you up, so wait for her right here, OK? I'll be back from work in time for dinner." She hesitates. "Unless you want me to leave work early and come get you? It's all right if you do. Or I could work from home today, in case you need to call me. Maybe I should tell my assistant that—"

"Mum, I'll be fine," I assure her. "You don't need to worry. I'll meet Dora here after school."

Mum purses her lips and takes a deep breath. "OK. I should leave you now."

I nod. She nods. We stand in silence for a few moments.

"Uh, Mum? You're gripping my shoulder VERY hard," I say.

"Sorry, sorry," she says, letting go and sniffing. "I knew this was going to be difficult but ... it's a little trickier than I imagined. At least you have Merlin looking over you."

"Mum, of all things to find comfort in, that is not one of them."

Merlin, in the form of a spider, peeks out from under my collar. "Don't worry, Aggie, I've got this."

"If you do anything to ruin this special day for Morgan," seethes Helena, sitting on Mum's shoulder as a ladybird, "I'll be very—"

"Boring!" Merlin interrupts, scuttling back under my collar. "Can we go in already?"

"Really!" Helena huffs. "There are some familiars who have no idea how lucky they are."

"If you need me, Morgan, you call, OK? Anything at all," Mum says sternly, before lowering her voice to a whisper. "And remember, no magic."

"Yeah, thanks, Mum. I think I remember that from the first ten billion times you've mentioned it. Now, you should go to the car and drive to work, and I'm going to go into the school," I say, gesturing to the yard. "I don't want to still be standing here when I'm a hundred and twenty years old."

"Good luck, darling!" she says.

I give her a little wave and watch as she collects herself, turns on her heel and marches to the car. Walking towards the school steps, I feel so nervous and excited at the same time – there's a lump in my throat and it feels like butterflies are having a Zumba lesson in my stomach. It's so noisy and everyone seems to know each other. I hope there are some other new kids starting this term so I'm not the only one.

"I just need to blend in," I tell myself under my breath, smiling broadly so that I look a lot more confident than I feel. "If I just blend in and act normal, I'll make friends in no time. This is it. This is my chance. Finally, I'm at school and I'm going to have friends! Actual friends!"

Suddenly, a football comes hurtling through the air and hits me right on the side of the head, making me lose my balance and go tumbling to the ground.

"Nicely done on blending in. I'm sure new friends will flock to you," Merlin grumbles in my ear, as I'm lying flat on my back. "You almost squashed me, genius."

A familiar face looms over mine as someone kneels next to me. "Hey! I thought I told you to stop banging your head."

Brilliant. Just brilliant.

Not only have I been knocked to the ground by a rogue football in front of EVERYONE as soon as I stepped through the gates, but of all people to be right there to witness it, it had to be Owen Blaze from that old bookshop. Because, of course, I haven't embarrassed myself in front of him enough.

"Are you OK?" he asks.

"I'm fine," I say hurriedly, as he helps me get to my feet. "Do you think anyone else saw?"

"Uh. . . " Owen looks around him at everyone in the yard staring right at us. "No, I think you're good."

I pick my bag off the ground as I rub the side of my head where the football struck. Owen's eyes flicker to the backpack and his forehead creases as he takes in the broomsticks, but he's kind enough not to say anything about it.

"My friend Felix over there has terrible aim when it comes to penalties," Owen tells me, gesturing to a tall, dark-haired boy who now has the football back and hasn't bothered to stop playing. "He kicked that pretty hard; are you sure you're all right?"

"I'm sure, thanks. OK, bye, Owen," I say, scurrying off and keeping my head down as my cheeks grow hot. The bell rings and there's a collective groan as everyone grabs their stuff and makes their way towards the school building.

"Whoa, whoa, wait up," Owen says with a laugh, falling into step with me. "So, we go to the same school! That's cool. It's Morgan, right? Is it your first day?"

"Yep."

"Do you know where you're going?"

"Yeah. Course," I lie, hoping he'll leave me alone. I just want to pretend the whole football thing never happened.

But walking into the main corridor, I stop as a mass of students bustles past me. This corridor appears to be the longest one in the world with lockers all the way down and lots of doors leading off it.

"Where are you supposed to be?" Owen asks, leading me to one side, out of everyone's way.

"The headmaster's office," I croak, retreating against the lockers as someone barges into my shoulder to get past. "Is it always this busy?"

"Yeah." He smiles. "Wasn't it like this at your old school? Or was it smaller there?"

"You could say that. I was home-schooled. There was just me."

He raises his eyebrows. "Seriously? So... is this the first time you've been to school? Ever?"

I nod, gulping.

"I guess this must seem a lot busier then." He laughs, before noticing someone come in through the doors. "There's Felix. Hey, Felix! Over here!"

He gestures at the boy who kicked the football to join us.

"This is Morgan," Owen says. "She's new. And you gave her a very warm welcome by giving her that red mark on the side of her forehead."

"Sorry about that," Felix says. He glances at my backpack and a smirk appears on his lips. "Nice bag."

"It's from Manningtree," I blurt out, when I can't think of anything else to say.

I hear a tiny sigh of despair from my left shoulder where Merlin is hidden.

"OK..." Felix says, staring at me in confusion.

"I don't know what Manningtree is. Is that, like, a brand?"

"No, it's . . . um . . . it's a town. In Essex. Never mind," I say quickly.

Fiddling nervously with my necklace, I try to think of something cool to say to make up for the stupid Manningtree comment. *Come on, brain, it's not that hard.* What do normal humans say on their first day of school when they first meet another normal human?

THINK, BRAIN, THINK.

"So," I begin, "do you go to school here?"

"Um. Yeah," Felix says slowly. "That's why I'm here. *At the school.*"

I hate my brain.

Felix turns to make a face at Owen which clearly means *is she stupid?!* But Owen seems way too amused by the whole exchange to notice.

"Right. Obviously," I squeak.

"Hey, guys!" Thankfully, a girl comes over to us and saves me from making any more stupid comments.

From the way she greets Owen and Felix, I think she must be in our year, but she looks a lot older and more sophisticated than us. She's tall and willowy, with curly dark hair and big, bright eyes framed by long, heavily mascaraed eyelashes.

The one time I tried mascara without using a spell to help me, Merlin was sitting in the empty bathtub waiting for me – in the form of a possum – and when I turned round, he literally *screamed* and then went, "Oh god, for a minute there I thought a spell had gone horribly wrong and you'd turned your eyes into spiders! But I see now you're just experimenting with make-up. Sorry, carry on."

The fact that this girl is wearing perfect make-up without any spells to help her is extremely impressive. I'm instantly intimidated by her.

"This is Morgan, she's new here," Felix says, before turning back to me with a thin-lipped smile. "Iris goes to this school, too. That's why she's here standing with us. In the school."

Iris looks confused and opens her mouth to say something, but stops suddenly, her eyes growing wide with horror as she stares at my shoulder.

"Wh–what … is … th–that?!" she says hoarsely, pointing a shaky finger at me.

"AAAARGH!" Felix cries, recoiling from me in disgust as Iris clutches his arm and backs away alongside him.

Everyone else in the corridor stops what they are doing and falls silent to look our way and see what all the fuss is about.

"Um, Morgan?" Owen says, frozen to the spot and nodding at my shoulder with a startled expression. "Don't panic, but ... are you OK with spiders?"

Oh no. This can't be happening. He wouldn't do this to me. HE SURELY WOULDN'T DO THIS TO ME ON MY FIRST DAY OF SCHOOL.

"Because," Owen continues in as calm a voice as he can muster, "I ... uh ... I think there's one on your shoulder. A quite big one."

"It's a TARANTULA!" Iris screams.

The corridor erupts into chaos. Students start screaming and racing in all directions, trying to get away.

During the panic, I hear a tiny voice on my shoulder go, "Well, hello, everyone!"

I hold up my hands quickly. "It's OK, everyone! It's OK! Nobody panic!"

"There is a TARANTULA ON YOU!" Felix repeats, just in case there was anyone left on the planet who hadn't heard the first time round.

"I know! I know, but it's OK. He's ... uh ... he's my pet tarantula. Yeah, he's my pet. So, no one needs to panic."

I smile at the sea of wide, repulsed eyes blinking back at me. No one says anything.

"I don't know how he got out of his cage this morning," I say, forcing a laugh. "Come here, you ... rascal."

I reach to get Merlin, but he ducks back under my collar and runs down my arm, under my sleeve. There is a ripple of gasps from our audience.

"He's in your clothes!" Iris shrieks. "GROSS!"

"Anyway," I croak, plastering on a fixed smile, "I'd better get going to the headmaster's office. Which is where I'm supposed to be."

Owen slowly lifts his arm and points at a set of doors down the corridor. "You go through there and up the stairs one floor. His office is on the first right."

"Great. Thank you. And no one needs to worry. I'll be taking my ... pet tarantula with me. He's safe and sound ... in my sleeve. OK, have a good first day of term everyone! Super excited to be here!"

The crowd parts as I make my way down the corridor, some people dramatically flattening themselves against the walls to get as far away from me as possible.

I push through the doors and reach the stairs, leaning against the bannister and burying my head in my hands, wishing I could click my fingers and disappear from this planet entirely.

"You know what they say," Merlin says smugly, scuttling out from my collar, "you should always make an entrance."

Chapter Six

"I don't understand why you're being so *boring* about this," Merlin sighs as I reach the top of the stairs. "Personally, I found the incident extremely entertaining! I'm almost certain that at least one of the students screaming their heads off peed themselves a little bit. I saw a wet patch on their trousers."

"Firstly, that's gross. Secondly, PLEASE can you just shut up and stay hidden?" I hiss, my heart sinking. "I haven't even been at this school for half an hour and you've already ruined everything. Do you know how much being here means to me?"

"You know, if you had any sense of humour, you'd be laughing about this and then helping me plot more tricks to play on these young children." He sniggers. "Think of what we could do!"

"Merlin," I say firmly, stopping at the door marked "HEADMASTER'S OFFICE". "I don't want to play tricks on these children. I want to be friends with them!"

"Typical, I have to be stuck with the most boring witch in history," he grumbles.

"Stay. Out. Of. Sight." I take a deep breath. "I'm in enough trouble as it is."

I knock on the door and hear someone call, "Come in!" from the other side. I push it open and straight ahead is a man in an ill-fitting suit seated at a small reception desk. On the desk there is a plaque reading "Headmaster's PA" and to my right is a large oak door, which I guess the headmaster's office is behind.

The PA is on the phone, looking very flustered.

"Oh yes, Mrs Smelton, we're doing all we can to... No, of course not, we'll be making sure... Absolutely, I completely understand... Well, let's not do anything irrational, Mrs Smelton... I know, and I'd like to talk that through with you, but please could you just hold the line one second—"

He presses a button to put her on hold, shuddering as he notices all the red flashing lights on his system that show calls waiting.

"Hi, I'm Morgan Charmley. It's my first day and I was told to come here to meet the headma—"

"What am I going to do? What am I going to do?" he cries out, ignoring me and running a hand through his hair so it sticks up messily. "It's a complete DISASTER!"

"Are you OK?"

"Am I OK? AM I OK? No, I'm not OK!" he yells, gesturing to the phone system blinking up at him. "These are all angry parents waiting to shout at me! And none of this is my fault!"

"Oh, well, I'm sure if you explain—"

"A deathly spider! On the loose! In our school!"

"What?" I squeak.

"There is a DEATHLY SPIDER IN THE SCHOOL! Oh god, what if we're shut down?" he says, on the brink of tears. "What if someone gets hurt and then we're shut down and I lose my job? WHAT HAPPENS THEN?"

"Ah, right," I say, as calmly as possible. "Look, I think I know what's happened here and actually there's no need to—"

"How are there more calls coming through?" he cries, pointing at the flashing lights. "The news is spreading! The news is spreading amongst the parents! I need to do some major crowd control!"

"Actually, I can—"

But he's already picked up the phone again, ignoring me. This could not get worse. And it's all Merlin's fault.

"Please," I say, coming right up to the desk to try and get his attention, "please listen and—"

"No, no, Mrs Smelton, it's all under control. . . Yes, I know, and she was right to ring you to let you know but we've got everything. . . No, Mrs Smelton, there really is no need for you to. . ."

I wave my hand under his nose. "I can actually expl—"

"Just go in!" he snaps, putting his hand over the receiver and pointing at the headmaster's door. "I have a lot to deal with right now!" He moves his hand and continues his attempts at calming Mrs Smelton.

Feeling like there's not much else I can do, I leave him panicking at his desk and walk towards the door, pushing it open and stepping into the room.

I regret it immediately.

I had wondered why the headmaster wasn't helping his assistant with the phone calls from terrified parents, but it turns out that he's got his music blaring so loudly in his office, you can't hear anything over it.

The headmaster, a tall, burly man wearing a navy-blue suit, is by his window, completely oblivious to the fact that I have come into his office. He is too busy salsa dancing with a teddy bear.

Yeah. I'm not kidding.

I stand frozen to the spot, mesmerized by the spectacle before me. His hips are swinging in time to the music, his feet pattering back and forth, and his eyes are closed as he holds a teddy bear paw in one hand, his other hand placed on the teddy's back.

Merlin has peeked out to see what's going on and starts howling with laughter.

"Shh!" I whisper, backing slowly towards the door, inch by inch.

I feel for the handle. If I can just get out of the office without the headmaster realizing and then knock before coming in, maybe everything will be all right.

Just as I've reached the handle and opened the door a fraction, the salsa song comes to an end and the headmaster finishes his steps with a great flourish, one arm up in the air, pretending to dip the teddy bear over his other arm.

He opens his eyes and sees me.

"AHHHHHHHHHHHHH!" he screams, throwing the teddy bear across the room.

"AHHHHHHHHHHHHHHH!" I scream at the same time because I wasn't expecting such a loud noise. "I'm so sorry! I didn't mean to—"

"What are you DOING in here?" he bellows, running to turn the music off as the next song starts playing. "Who are you?"

"I-I'm so sorry. I'm Morgan Charmley. I was told to come and see you; it's my first day!"

"Why didn't you *knock*?"

"I am asking myself that very same question," I squeak. "I'm really sorry."

We're both silent. My face feels like it's on fire and I have no idea what to do. The headmaster is flustered, breathing heavily with his brow furrowed.

"I think," he says eventually, in a forced-calm voice, "the best thing to do is for you to go out of the office, knock and then come back in again. And we just pretend . . . we just pretend this never ever happened."

I nod. "OK. That sounds good to me."

"You didn't see me practising my salsa dancing with the school mascot teddy bear," he says, staring me down.

"No, I . . . uh . . . I didn't see that."

"We're on the same page?"

"Absolutely."

"You see, if other students were to hear about this then I might lose my . . . carefully constructed air of authority," he says, clearly feeling the need to explain himself. "Now, you are under no obligation to keep this secret, but I—"

"Seriously," I say quickly, holding up my hands, "nothing has happened. I'm just going to go out of the office and then I'm going to knock on the door."

"Good. Yes. That would be good."

I spin round and open the door, hurrying through it and then slamming my back against it as I pull it shut.

"Oh. My. God," I say out loud, closing my eyes as tightly as possible.

"This is the best day of my life," Merlin says cheerily on my shoulder. "Now I understand why witches should go to school. It is filled with painful humiliation! This is so FUN!"

I open my eyes to see the headmaster's assistant still fielding calls from parents. He hasn't even noticed that I've come back through the door and is now talking to a Mr Elliot, assuring him that the school is doing everything in its power to get the "spider situation" under control.

After a few moments of watching him, worrying that he might be about to combust from stress, I knock VERY loudly on the headmaster's door.

I hear him clear his throat. "Come in!"

I push open the door for the second time and poke my head through.

"Ah, Miss Charmley," he says from his seat behind his desk. "Do come and sit down."

I scuttle across the office and sit on the chair opposite him, sinking deeply into it.

"Welcome to Riddle House School. I'm Mr Hopkins, the headmaster. I see from your files that you were home-schooled up until now, yes?"

"Yes," I say quietly, unable to look him in the eye.

"Well, I'm sure you won't have a problem settling into our lively and excellent school. My assistant will be able to give you all the information you need about your form and your timetable. When you leave here, just stop by his desk and ask for all the details." He shifts in his seat. "Do you . . . have any questions you'd like to ask?"

I shake my head firmly. I have never felt so uncomfortable.

"Great! Well, that's all done then." He jumps to his feet. "Off you go and have a really good first day."

As I stand up, ready to escape, the door swings open and the assistant enters with a furious expression.

"Ah, Andrew, I was just instructing Morgan here to get her timetable from you so she can be on her way," Mr Hopkins says. "No need for her to hang around here, eh, Morgan?"

"*You!*" Andrew snarls, lifting a shaky finger to point at me. "You are the one behind all this."

"Andrew, what's going on?" Mr Hopkins asks, looking confused. "That vein on your forehead looks as though it might burst! Everything all right?"

"No, headmaster, everything is NOT all right," he croaks, still pointing at me.

I gulp. "I should probably be getting to my first lesson, so—"

"NOT so fast!" Andrew cries, barricading the door. "Where is it?"

"Andrew, I demand to know what's going on!" Mr Hopkins says, coming out from behind his desk.

"Headmaster, while you have been in here, I have been fielding *hundreds* of phone calls," Andrew explains, his voice switching from angry to wobbly. "Parents are out of their minds because THIS new student has brought in a DEATHLY SPIDER!"

Mr Hopkins gasps and stumbles backwards, clutching the side of his desk.

"This is all a big misunderstanding," I say quickly. "There's no deathly spider and there's really no reason for panic. I think someone saw a spider and they got a bit freaked out and then, you know how it is. Things get . . . blown out of proportion." I shrug, smiling at Mr

Hopkins and Andrew. "Really, there is nothing to worry about."

"B-but," Andrew stammers in reply, looking ashen-faced, "on y-your sh-shoulder."

OH, COME ON. He cannot be doing this to me AGAIN!

I look out of the corner of my eye and see Merlin perched happily in full view, and to make matters worse, he's decided to become a much bigger tarantula than he was earlier. He lifts one of his legs in greeting at Andrew and then Mr Hopkins.

Andrew screams at the top of his lungs.

"WHAT IS THAT?" Mr Hopkins shrieks. "AND WHY IS IT WAVING AT ME?"

"It's OK, it's OK," I assure them. "I lied! I'm sorry, I lied! So I have a tarantula but he's completely harmless. Really. He would never hurt a fly!"

It just so happens that a small fly buzzes towards my shoulder at that exact moment. Merlin opens his spider jaws and clamps his fangs down over it.

WHAT. ARE. THE. CHANCES.

Andrew faints and collapses on to the floor. Mr Hopkins whimpers, retreating to hide behind his desk.

"Mr Hopkins, wait, there really is no need to panic. This is my pet tarantula and he's very well behaved. I don't know what happened this morning, but he must have got out of his cage. Don't panic though, I have a little cage with me! In my backpack. For emergencies, like this one."

"Y-you do?" Mr Hopkins squeaks. He's ducked so low behind the desk that I can just see a tuft of his hair.

"Yes, I do," I tell the tuft. "I'll just pop him in the cage and the problem is solved. He won't be seen by any students for the rest of the day. I *promise*."

"All right, then. I never want to see that KILLER THING on school premises ever AGAIN," he emphasizes, attempting to keep the tremors out of his voice.

"Of course." I hesitate, feeling the need to defend the species that my familiar is attempting to discredit. "Um, actually, just so you know, tarantulas are quite docile by nature. Yeah, they've got a bit of a bad reputation because of films and I guess they look a bit frightening, but really they would only bite you if they felt provoked. And even then, the venom isn't that harmful to—"

"GET. OUT!"

An arm protrudes from behind the desk and points at the door.

"Sure, yeah, OK, I should leave."

I get to the door and pause, looking down at Andrew sprawled across the carpet.

"Should I ... do you want me to get him some water or something?"

"*Miss Charmley*," the shaky voice behind the desk begins, "I suggest you and your *pet* get to your classroom immediately. I know it's only your first day but ... you are on your FINAL WARNING!"

Chapter Seven

Whispers follow me all the way down the classroom to a desk at the back where there's a spare seat.

"Yeah, that's her. She brought her *tarantula* to school."

"EW! I heard it lives in her sleeve!"

"I heard she was carrying it around in her hair!"

"Apparently there was more than one spider!"

"I heard there were three!"

"No, she had two tarantulas in her hair and a gecko on her shoulder!"

"Who brings a gecko to school? So weird!"

"Who brings a TARANTULA to school?"

"What a FREAK!"

I slide into my seat and the boy sitting next to me

shuffles his seat as far away as possible. He flattens himself against the wall, staring at me wide-eyed.

"Hi," I whisper, smiling brightly. "I'm Morgan."

He blinks at me and doesn't say anything.

"Don't worry," I say, forcing a laugh. "I don't have a tarantula up my sleeve. He's safe and sound in my locker."

He wrinkles his nose in disgust, still not saying anything, before turning to look straight ahead of him, his body angled away from me.

"Want me to turn into a piranha and bite his butt?" Merlin whispers into my ear, now in the form of a smaller spider.

I turn my head towards Merlin as subtly as possible and, without moving my lips, say through my teeth like some kind of ventriloquist, *"No, I do not!* Just stay hidden!"

I turn back to see the boy watching me suspiciously. I shoot him a big, enthusiastic smile. He does not smile back.

"Right, let's get started," Miss Campbell, our history teacher, says cheerily, clapping her hands. "What an exciting year ahead, so much wonderful history to study and discuss! I don't know about you, but I can't WAIT to get started."

She turns to the board and starts writing "What is

History?" in big letters across it. I spot Owen on the other side of the classroom sitting next to Felix. Owen is opening his notepad, while Felix looks bored out of his mind already. He looks around the classroom, distracted, and sees me watching them. Mortified, I quickly pretend to focus on getting my pencil case from my backpack.

"Hey, Morgan," Felix calls out, a smile creeping across his face, "is the tarantula still up your sleeve? Or are you keeping it in that really cool *witch* backpack of yours?"

There is a ripple of sniggers across the class. Everyone has swivelled round in their seats to stare at me. Miss Campbell stops writing and turns to us with a look of confusion.

My cheeks flame as I feel everyone's eyes on me. The classroom is totally silent and I try desperately to think of something to say, but I also know that if I open my mouth to speak I won't be able to hold back my tears. This is completely new to me.

Normally, it takes a lot to make me cry. It's not like I'm not used to being on my own and dealing with abnormal incidents. Two years ago, I was trying out this new spell to turn my hair pink that Dora had been teaching me and I clicked my fingers and . . .

. . . somehow turned my hair and eyebrows into worms. WORMS. A HEAD OF WORMS. And two worms

ON MY FACE ACTING AS EYEBROWS.

And Mum was downstairs talking to a neighbour who had popped by for a cup of tea so I had to wait an HOUR until she could come upstairs and fix it.

But I didn't cry once. Not at all.

In fact, within that hour I grew weirdly attached to the worms and gave all of them names. I even asked the one above my right eyebrow if she could switch places with Merlin and become my familiar but sadly that wasn't possible.

Anyway, that's just one example of how difficult it is to make me cry.

But I suppose all the events of this morning, ever since I stepped through the school gates, have been piling up and this last snide comment from Felix combined with so many people staring at me as though I don't belong there is enough to tip me over the edge.

"Why do you want to know where the tarantula is, Felix?" Owen says suddenly, making everyone turn to look at him instead. "You screamed so loudly the first time you saw it, I think a second time might make you faint on the spot."

The class bursts out laughing and Felix frowns at his friend before quietly muttering, "I did NOT scream."

"All right, enough please," Miss Campbell says, clearing her throat. "Let's focus. Felix, don't disrupt my class again. I don't want us to have a repeat of last year when you achieved a record number of lunchtime detentions, got it?"

Felix shrugs and Miss Campbell gestures to the board before launching into an introduction to the lesson. I glance over at Owen, who catches my eye. I smile gratefully at him. He smiles back.

When the bell signals the end of the lesson, the boy next to me grabs his stuff and literally *runs away*. "You know," Merlin whispers in my ear as I put my pens back in my pencil case, "I once heard of a familiar in Bulgaria, who was so angry at some kids bullying his witch, he transformed into a huge buffalo and stampeded through the school, charging right at them. Apparently, those bullies were so frightened they never spoke again. Ever. Just say the word, Morgan, and anyone who makes fun of you will be a goner."

"Wow," I reply, hiding my face with my hair as I duck down to grab my backpack. "I think that may be the sweetest thing you've ever said to me. But if it's all right with you, I'd rather you didn't trample any of these people. I'm kind of hoping I'll be friends with them.

Eventually."

Merlin snorts. "Yeah, good luck with that."

"Things will get better," I say confidently, slinging my backpack over my shoulder and getting up from my chair. "They have to."

Things did not get better. In fact, things got distinctly worse.

The tarantula rumour got so out of control that by lunchtime, I overheard someone saying that I was running an illegal spider farm from my locker. And the only time anyone spoke to me all morning was when a boy in the year above came over to ask me if it was true that I'd been expelled from my last school for letting a snake loose in the library.

Lunch was the worst bit of the day. At least in lessons, you are assigned a seat and you have to focus on the teacher, so it's not as obvious that everyone is avoiding you. But lunch breaks make your social status in the school hierarchy crystal clear. I had nowhere to sit and no one to sit with, and I stood at the side of the canteen for ages working out what on earth to do. Eventually, I took my tray out of the canteen and sat on my own in the library.

"I went through exactly the same thing during my

first week at school," Dora assures me in the car on the way home when school finishes for the day.

"Really? You're not just saying that to be nice?"

"Honest! It took me a long time to make any friends. I think it was because I was actually quite a shy child. That, and maybe the vomiting thing."

"What vomiting thing?"

"Oh, it wasn't a big deal," she says, waving off the question.

"Not a big deal!" Mac laughs loudly, lying across the backseats in corgi form. "She was so nervous that she projectile vomited over the headmaster on her first day."

"You *what*? OK," I say with a laugh, "that makes me feel a little better. Maybe there is some hope for me to make friends."

"Although Dora was five years old, remember," Merlin points out, in the form of a crow sitting on my head. "That's young enough to get away with embarrassing stuff like that. You, on the other hand, are thirteen. It's not the same."

"Thanks for making me feel better, Merlin," I sigh, looking out of the window.

We come to a stop at the traffic lights and there is a group of older students from the school walking down the pavement towards the bus stop. One of them does a double take at me and then gestures to the others to look, too. They look completely stunned.

At first I think that maybe they heard the spider rumours and that's why they're pointing and staring, and then I realize what I must look like to them.

Sitting in the front seat with a BIRD CHILLING ON MY HEAD.

"MERLIN!" I cry, sliding as far down in my seat as possible. "Is there any way you can transform into anything else? Those girls can see you and it looks so odd!"

"I can't! If I disappear and transform into something else, they'll see the magic," he argues. "I have to stay in this form."

"Why aren't these lights going green?" I groan.

"I have an idea!" Dora says, seeing my predicament. "Mac, turn into a bird and come sit on my head! If both of us are doing it, you won't look so strange, Morgan."

"What? No! Mac don't—" I begin, but he has already transformed into a pigeon and flown to land on her head.

"There!" Dora says with great satisfaction. "They'll see that I have a pigeon on my head. It's not just you."

"Yes, good one," Merlin says gleefully. "Now, Morgan doesn't look strange at *all*."

The lights change to green and we set off down the

road, the students huddled together and crying with laughter. At least they were too stunned to reach for their phones in time to take photos.

"There's no need to worry, Morgan," Dora says cheerfully as we pull into the driveway. "Things will get much better as the week goes on. You'll see."

But I soon found out Dora was wrong. The damage was done.

Even though Merlin was on good behaviour for the rest of the week and stayed hidden away, no one seemed interested in making friends with me. I still had no one to sit next to at lunchtimes and people would whisper horrible things about me when I passed them in the corridor. Examples include: "weirdo"; "she's so strange"; "freak alert"; and there's this one boy in the year below me who insists on jumping away from me so dramatically any time we walk past each other that the first time he sprained his ankle and the second time he almost broke his wrist when he slammed his hand against the wall. The way people act around me, you'd think I had some kind of contagious disease.

And it wasn't like I was enjoying lessons either, because I was so behind on everything. I've been working so hard towards the YWE recently, that my normal-school studying fell behind a little bit. Everything was a complete disaster and when the week FINALLY came to an end, I was wondering why on earth I'd been so desperate to come to school in the first place. How was I ever going to fit in?

"Hey, Morgan. What are you up to this weekend?"

I jump as Owen suddenly appears next to me on Friday afternoon, just as I'm transferring all my books from my locker into my backpack. On my second day at school, I worked out a system of switching everything from my witch backpack in the mornings to a plain blue backpack, which I use at school. Then just before Dora picks me up, I switch it back again so she thinks I'm using her one and I don't have to hurt her feelings.

"Not much, just normal weekend stuff," I say, thinking about how I'll be having my first broomstick-flying lesson at midnight with Dora and Mum. "What about you?"

"Not much, just normal stuff." He grins before nodding at Iris who walks past with some friends. "Iris has organized for a group of us to go to the cinema tomorrow. Want to come?"

"Uh. I don't think I should."

"Why not?"

I hesitate. "Why are you being nice to me?"

"What do you mean?"

I shut my locker and begin walking down the corridor with him. "I mean, why are you being nice? You don't have to be. Isn't everyone going to think you're weird if you're talking to me? And there's no way anyone would want me to come along to the cinema. I haven't exactly got off to a great start here."

"No one does." He shrugs. "You know Felix once wet himself at school?"

"WHAT?"

I'm so shocked by what Owen is saying that I'm staring at him rather than looking where I'm going, and I walk straight into the headmaster, who is coming down the corridor the other way.

When he sees it's me, his face clouds over.

"Miss Charmley," he seethes. "Watch where you are going."

"S-sorry, Mr Hopkins," I squeak.

He walks around me, glaring as he goes.

"Whoa," Owen comments, watching his back as he disappears through the doors. "He really does not like you."

"Tell me about it." I sigh. "Him and everyone else at this school. Anyway, what were you saying about Felix wetting himself?"

"Oh yeah." He laughs. "It was when we were little

– we were at the junior school together. But most people have forgotten about that, so it will be the same for you. And Iris may be popular now, but when she first came here she hardly said a word. Everyone thought she was really cold and superior. But she was just shy."

"Iris was shy?" I shake my head in disbelief. "She's the most confident girl in school! As far as I can tell, anyway."

"Yeah, well, not at first. School is always rubbish for a bit when you're new."

"All the other new students have settled in nicely. Then again, they didn't bring a tarantula to school," I admit, holding open the door for us and heading down the steps.

"I think the tarantula thing was kind of cool. Weird, but cool weird."

I give him a small smile. "Thanks. It's nice of you to try to make me feel better. But maybe I need to think about going back to being home-schooled."

"Morgan," Owen says, stopping at the school gates, "it's only been one week. You can't give up straight away."

"I suppose."

"What did you think it was going to be like?" He grins. "Did you think that you'd just be able to click your fingers and make everything perfect?"

Chapter Eight

"Are you excited?" Mum asks as Dora fetches the broomsticks from the boot of the car.

"Not really," I say, watching a ball of dim white light float past me through the air.

As it's pitch black at night, Mum has cast a spell so that we have these small lights floating around us all the time. Merlin turned into a grasshopper and tried to leap on to one from my shoulder, but it swiftly dodged him and he fell to the ground, much to Helena's amusement.

He's now back on my shoulder, tucked under my jumper as a beetle pretending to sleep, but I know he's sulking.

Mum is surprised by my lack of enthusiasm and bursts into laughter. "Morgan, you must be the only witch I've ever met who isn't excited for their first broomstick-flying lesson! I was itching to get on a broomstick back when I passed my YWE."

"Yeah, of course you were!" I sigh. "Hello! Have you met you? You're good at everything! I'm terrible at everything, particularly anything practical or sporty. And anything that involves good coordination. Don't you remember the time that you tried to teach me how to play tennis?"

Mum winces at the memory.

In my defence, I didn't INTEND on swinging my arm too fast and letting the tennis racket slip from my grip so that it hurtled into her stomach.

Tennis is a stupid game.

"That was different," she says firmly. "You don't need to be sporty or have good coordination to fly a broomstick."

"Yes, you do! I'm going to need to dodge around trees and other such obstacles!"

"That's the same as walking!"

"Walking doesn't involve flying through the air at great speed!"

"Oh darling, don't be so nervous." Mum smiles, putting an arm around me. "We'll go nice and slowly at first. You're going to be a natural, I can tell."

But just because Mum was a natural does not mean I'm going to be one. Mum is like the witches you read about in books or see in films (the good witches, anyway). She's just naturally brilliant at almost everything; she was *born* to be a witch. She's special. She is exactly the sort of witch you would entrust with a special trinket or a dangerous but noble quest.

I, on the other hand, am not that kind of witch. I'm the kind that books and films either don't show, or if they do, it's simply to make the main witch of the plot look better by comparison.

I once expressed feeling this way to Merlin.

His response was, "That's probably why you're so sarcastic. You use humour to hide all your flaws. But you're not very funny, so it's like a double whammy of shortcomings. Anyway, can we go watch that new *Transformers* movie now? I'm bored."

So, that was very enlightening.

"Here we go," Dora says enthusiastically, coming over to us with three broomsticks. "Morgan, you must be so excited! I couldn't wait to get on my first broomstick!"

"The clearing is just up here," Mum says in her mystical, authoritative Great Sorceress voice, leading the way down the woodland path. "For centuries, witches have used this very spot to learn how to fly. It's out of the way and there's plenty of space."

"Witches cast a spell on this clearing in the sixteenth century," Dora tells me excitedly, as sticks and twigs crack under our feet. "They made sure no trees could grow here, so as to keep it a good space for learning how to fly. It's confused non-witches for years! They think it's something to do with the soil."

"Here we are," Mum says, leading us into the centre of a circle of trees. "This brings back memories, eh, Dora?"

"Oh yes." Dora chuckles. "I went bottom first into that tree right there. Turned out, the broomstick was in reverse! I wonder if the dent still exists?"

"How did you not know the broomstick was in reverse?" I gulp as Dora examines the tree. "Are there gears and stuff? I don't think I can handle gears. I don't even understand bike gears. Mum, I don't think I'm ready for this. We should go home."

"You're ready, Morgan, and Dora shouldn't be making you more nervous by telling you about silly little accidents," she says, giving Dora a stern look. "Dora was thinking about the broomstick being in reverse before she took off, and that's why she went backwards."

"That's right." Dora nods. "I was distracted by

imagining what would happen if the broomstick was in reverse. I soon found out."

"Here." Mum passes me a broomstick. "Get on."

"Straight away?"

"How else do you think you learn?"

"I don't know, isn't there a theory exam first?"

"It's not something you can learn from a book," Mum says, as Dora passes us a broomstick each. They both get on theirs and wait for me to follow suit.

I nervously hold the end of the broomstick and then, after collecting myself, I step over it.

"Well done!" Mum cries enthusiastically.

"Mum. I'm just holding it. Nothing has happened."

"Yes, but that's the first step," she says cheerily.

"You look very becoming on that broomstick," Dora says, her eyes filling with tears. "I can't b-believe how grown-up you look! You're a proper witch!"

"I feel a bit stupid."

"Well, of course you do," Mum says. "Look at you! You look ridiculous."

"Thanks, Mum."

"But once you're up in the air, you will look elegant and regal. There's no feeling like flying," Mum says wistfully, gazing up at the stars. "Now, flying is all in the mind. You need to focus. Clear your mind of everything else."

"Whatever you do," Dora adds, "don't think about ponds."

"What? WHY would I think about ponds?"

"Well, *I* was thinking about a pond during my first flying lesson, because we'd been learning about the life cycle of frogs that day at school. Anyway, it was in my brain and then I flew right into one. Head first, unlike the tree incident," she says with a chuckle, before hesitating. "No wait. I think I flew bottom first into the pond, too."

"*Anyway,*" Mum says, glaring at her, "as I was saying, Morgan, you simply need to clear your mind of everything. Just calmly breathe in and focus on the here and now."

I inhale deeply, shutting my eyes.

"Very good," Mum says softly. "Is your mind clear?"

"Honestly," I sigh, "all I can think about now is ponds."

"What did I JUST tell you?" Dora tuts, shaking her head. "Aren't you paying attention?"

"It was YOU who put ponds in my head in the first place!"

"All right." Mum holds up her hands. "No more talk of ponds. Let's try to get through this first lesson by the next century. Morgan, follow my breathing. That's it, very good. Inhale ... and exhale ... and inhale ... very good. Now, I want you to think of flying, and nothing else. That broomstick is completely under your control. It's on your side. It wants to help you."

I swallow the lump in my throat and stare down at the broomstick handle, wondering if it can read my mind, because Mum is speaking as though it can.

Which is creepy.

"And then," she continues, "you click your fingers and up you g—"

"How can I hold on to the broom if I click my fingers?" I ask in a panic.

"You hold on with your other hand. You click your fingers just like with all spells."

"I need to hold on with both hands."

"That's OK," Mum says, very slowly and calmly, "you can click your fingers and then grab the broomstick as soon as you've clicked. It's not as hard as it sounds."

"It doesn't sound that hard," Merlin comments, transforming into a wasp and buzzing in my ear. I swat him away.

"It's natural to be nervous the first time," Mac says in the form of a hummingbird, hovering over Dora's shoulder. "You're doing great, Morgan."

"Thanks, Mac. You're such an encouraging and kind familiar," I say pointedly.

"Are you ready?" Mum asks gently, smiling at me.

"I guess so. I breathe deeply, focus, and then will the broomstick to fly as I click my fingers."

"That's pretty much it," Dora says happily.

"Whenever you're ready, Morgan," Mum says.

They both kick off the ground and hover in the air on their broomsticks, making it look really easy.

I try to push away the nerves. I try to imagine what it's like to fly. I try not to think about diving accidentally into ponds. I try to tell myself that I'm not a completely useless witch and maybe, just maybe, there is a chance I won't completely mess this up.

I click my fingers.

Nothing happens.

"Nothing's happened," Merlin points out.

"Yeah, thanks, Merlin, I noticed that," I snap. "How is that possible? I was really calm and focused!"

"Morgan." Mum chuckles. "How many witches do you think get it the first time?"

"Did you get it the first time?"

"Yes," she says reluctantly. "But that was luck and it's very rare."

"It took me plenty of tries to get up in the air," Dora

reassures me. "And once I did, well ... you've heard the pond and tree stories."

"Shall we try again?" Mum suggests.

I sigh, shrugging as my eyes fall to the ground. "I guess so."

"Morgan," she says in a firm voice, forcing me to look up at her, "you can do this. It doesn't matter how long it takes; I know you can do this. There's only one reason it might not work for a while. Do you know what that is?"

I shake my head.

"It's because you don't believe you can. It was the same with your YWE. This has nothing to do with your ability, it's all to do with your confidence and your belief in yourself."

"Your mum is right." Dora smiles. "I wasn't lying earlier. You really do look like a proper witch on that broomstick. You've passed your YWE now, Morgan. *You're ready.*"

They're both looking at me so earnestly, I can't help but believe them a tiny bit. Yeah, so I'm not the most disciplined and in-control witch but I've worked really hard recently AND even when my spells go wrong, they are still powerful.

Like turning Dora into a turnip. Or turning that boy into a toad. Or turning my hair into worms.

That's got to count for something. Right?

I grip my broomstick determinedly. I clear my brain of everything else. I am a witch. A proper witch and it's about time that I fly like one.

I click my fingers.

Suddenly, I'm jolted up, my feet lifting into the air, and I hover about two feet off the ground.

"OH MY GOD!" I scream, realizing that I am ACTUALLY IN THE AIR.

The spell is broken and I drop to the ground, falling off my broomstick and lying flat on my back amongst the mud and the leaves. Mum and Dora land, step off their broomsticks and come running over. I beam up at them. I've never felt so elated in all my life.

"Are you all right?" Dora asks, tears of joy running down her face as she helps Mum pull me to my feet.

"Oh, Morgan," Mum says, looking as though she might burst with pride as she pulls leaves and twigs out of my hair, "you did it!"

"Yeah," I say with a laugh, bending down to pick my broomstick off the ground. "I did!"

Chapter Nine

I wish I could talk to someone about my flying lessons.

I know I have Mum and Dora, but it's not quite the same as getting excited about it with someone my own age. Mum keeps encouraging me to try to make friends with this young witch, Sandy, who lives in a village nearby, but I don't think that's going to happen. We met a couple of years ago when her mum invited me over as a favour to my mum, and when I told her that I hadn't passed my YWE yet so I wasn't at school, she folded her arms and went, "Wow, you must be *really* bad at spells," in this snooty voice.

So I accidentally clicked my fingers and turned her into a cactus.

And let me just say that there is nothing funnier than

a cactus wearing a purple dress screaming, "Mummy! Mummy! Look what she did!"

I obviously got grounded and received ANOTHER lecture from Mum about how I shouldn't turn people who are mean to me into things like cacti or toads. I told her that Sandy started the whole thing and I was merely proving to her that I was NOT bad at spells, but Mum wouldn't listen.

Anyway, every now and then Mum will say, "How about I invite Sandy and her mum over for tea this weekend? Wouldn't it be nice to have a witch friend your own age?"

And I always have to reply something along the lines of, "Hey, good idea, except, remember that time I turned her into a cactus?"

Mum thinks Sandy will have forgiven me by now, but to be honest, even if she has, I haven't forgiven HER for saying I was bad at spells. It's a lost cause.

Still, it would be nice to be able to talk about the flying stuff with someone who gets it. I've had a few lessons now and it is SO much fun. I'm definitely not a natural, but I'm really learning. In my last lesson, I flew above the trees of the clearing in a neat circle and came in to land quite smoothly. The landing part is what I'm finding the hardest. It takes a lot of control and mostly

I just end up hovering a bit and then toppling off my broom.

I could not be more grateful for my weekend flying lessons right now. They are the only thing keeping me going through this school term.

School hasn't got any better since the first week. I've tried to go up to people and start speaking to them, so they can see that I'm nice and don't have tarantulas hiding up my sleeve ready to attack them or crows perching on my head, but most people avoid me.

By far my worst lesson at school is P.E. It seems so unfair that we are forced into sport when some of us are not inclined that way. Do they make the non-musical students have music lessons? No. Do they make the non-drama students act on stage? No.

So WHY do they force non-sporty students to play sport in front of other kids?!

I get that exercise is good for you and all that, but I would *really* appreciate it if the teachers separated us into groups reflecting our abilities so I wouldn't have to suffer this constant humiliation. They could let the sporty students like Owen, Felix and Iris compete against each other and participate in team sports or whatever, and then they could let the fitness-challenged students like me just get on with some nice, light exercises in another room all by ourselves, so no one has to see.

Unfortunately, that is not how it works.

"MORGAN CHARMLEY!" yells our sports teacher, Mrs Fernley, almost giving me a heart attack. "Why have you stopped? You can't be taking another break? You haven't even done one lap yet! Iris is about to lap you!"

"I was ... uh ... checking my shoelace," I wheeze, leaning against a tree.

She puts her hands on her hips. "And is your shoelace all in order?"

I look down at my double-knotted shoelaces. "Uh. Yes. It looks good."

"Then off you go! Come on," she says, clapping her hands. "Go! Go! GO!"

I reluctantly push myself off the tree and force myself to keep going, even though my legs feel like jelly and I have a stitch. How is running round a field a warm-up? It is *cold* outside! It doesn't make any sense!

"Very good, Iris!" I hear Mrs Fernley call out as Iris glides past me. "Your running has improved so much; what an inspiration to us all!"

When I reach the end of my second lap, everyone else is huddled together, stretching and chatting happily. Another girl in our class, Jenny, arrives just ahead of me and is bent over double catching her breath, not exactly a sporting woman herself. Last week I tried talking to her about it, but my bonding attempt didn't go very well.

"Is your ankle OK, Jenny?" I asked in the changing rooms, after she'd twisted it during a hockey lesson. We were the last ones in there.

As with everyone else, she looked a bit scared that I was talking directly to her.

I've got used to this reaction.

"Um, it's fine, thanks," she murmured, hurrying to get her shoes on.

"I hate P.E.," I said, imagining she might agree. But she didn't say anything, so I continued. "It's hard being the worst, right?"

She looked up at me. "What?"

"It's hard, isn't it, to be the worst."

"Are ... are you saying I'm the worst at P.E.?" Her eyes filled up with tears.

"No! No, I was saying, *I'm* the worst at P.E.! And you're ... uh ... well, you're—"

"I get it, I'm awful at running and sports and I just shouldn't bother trying," she sniffed, standing up and grabbing her bag. "Everyone is just laughing at me, aren't they!"

And then she stormed out before I could explain myself.

"I think the trick to making friends is to be nice to them." Merlin smirked. "Rather than offend them and give them a complex that they'll have hanging over them the rest of their lives.".

Ever since that incident, Jenny has pretended I don't exist. She just looks right past me. And actually, now that I think about it, I'd rather be invisible. Especially to people like Felix.

"Finally," Felix sighs, as I reach the group and start my stretches. "Now that Morgan has finished her warm-up, the lesson is over."

Most of the class burst out laughing, even though his joke isn't that funny. I keep my eyes to the ground, ignoring him, but when I glance up I notice that Iris is looking at him disapprovingly. I must have imagined it though, because Iris isn't exactly my biggest fan. She hasn't spoken to me or acknowledged my existence since the tarantula episode on the first day.

"Do you want to do another lap, Felix?" Mrs Fernley asks, frowning at him. "Any more comments from you and that's what you'll be doing while we're all having fun. Right, everyone, today I'll be splitting you into small groups to practise some hockey drills and then you can play a team game at the end of the lesson."

"Let's hope we're not stuck with Jenny or Morgan," I hear Felix whisper loudly to the boy standing next to him.

I try not to let him get to me, pushing my hands into my pockets and thinking instead about my flying lesson this coming weekend. He is making it increasingly hard not to turn him into a toad or a cactus, though.

"Before we get started, I have an exciting announcement to make," Mrs Fernley says brightly. "As you all know, you are now old enough to partake in the school talent show at the end of term!"

Several students let out squeals of excitement and Iris high-fives Lucy, the girl standing next to her. Owen looks about as impressed as I feel at this news.

"And this year, we've made it *compulsory* for Year Nines."

"WHAT?" Felix snorts. "I'm not taking part in a stupid talent show!"

"You only think it's stupid because you don't have any talents," Iris teases, making everyone laugh.

Mrs Fernley clears her throat. "As I was saying, we have decided to make the talent show compulsory for your year. There are many reasons why Mr Hopkins has made this decision. He thought it would be an excellent opportunity for teamwork, to try new things and to get creative. The reason I am telling you this news now rather than leaving it to your form teacher is because I am hoping that some of you might consider doing a gymnastics or dance routine, or something else sports-related. If you do want to do something along those lines, please report to me in your groups and I can organize a timetable so you can book the gym hall for rehearsals."

"This is rubbish," Felix groans loudly. "We have to do this in our free time?"

"Yes, Felix, because it's *fun* and forces you all to tear your eyes away from your phones for once. It's only for the term and who knows? You may enjoy it!"

Iris's hand shoots up. "Our group would like to speak to you about doing a dance routine, Mrs Fernley. Can we book in our rehearsal slots now before anyone else takes up the best times?"

"Ah, well, you don't know your group yet."

Iris looks confused. "What do you mean? We've already formed our group. We were going to enter the competition even if it wasn't compulsory."

"You will be put into groups," Mrs Fernley replies simply, looking down at her clipboard.

"We can't choose our own groups?" Iris's jaw drops

to the floor as Lucy grabs her hand in fear. "But . . . how will that work?"

"I have a list here with all the groups which your form teacher has put together, and at the end of the lesson I'll stick it up on the noticeboard. You can see who you're with, then. This is a good thing! It will challenge you to incorporate all your various talents, and see what each individual can bring. Now"– she points to the row of hockey sticks – "let's get on with the lesson."

Merlin, in the form of a wasp hovering by my ear, says exactly what I'm thinking. "As if you weren't hating school enough, they're forcing you to be in a talent show."

After a humiliating five minutes during which no one picks me for their hockey team and then when Mrs Fernley assigns me to a side, they start arguing about having to take me, pleading with the other side to take the hit, I spend the next forty minutes dodging the ball any time it rolls in my direction. The bell finally rings and we're ushered off the field and into the changing rooms. There's a mad rush as the enthusiastic talent-show fans race to get ready and see the group listing on the board.

Mrs Fernley waits until everyone has come out of the changing room before pinning the list to the board and then running away to shut herself in her office before the complaining starts.

There are so many people huddled round the board that it takes me ages to get close enough to see what group I'm in.

"You're kidding," Iris groans at the front.

"What are we going to do?" Lucy whines.

I guess they didn't get put in the same group and at first I feel a bit sorry for them, considering they had already worked on a dance routine together or whatever. But then I remember that yesterday Lucy purposefully ignored me when I asked her a question after class, before whispering "she is such a *loser*" in my earshot as I walked away, and then I don't feel sorry for her in the slightest.

I wait patiently for the crowd to subside as everyone leaves to get to our next lesson, and then I sidle up to the board.

Oh no.

When I see my name, I shut my eyes tight and then open them again to make sure I'm not imagining it.

Nope. There it is. Still in that group.

"It could be worse," Merlin whispers to me, in the form of a ladybird.

"*How* could this be worse?" I ask, burying my head in my hands.

He hesitates. "Uh . . . hmm . . . no, you're right. This couldn't be worse."

<u>GROUP THREE</u>
Iris Beckett
Kareen Samara
Zoey McAlister
Lucy Chan
Morgan Charmley

Chapter Ten

"So, is there anything that you *can* do?" Iris asks me
in exasperation.

What I want to say is: "Yes, Iris. Not only do I
have the magical ability to turn you all into toads, I
have also recently learned how to fly on a broomstick.
And hey, if you REALLY want to win that talent show,
how about I cast a few spells over the judges so that
they'll crown us the winners no matter what we do?
Because I have the power to do that, just by clicking
my fingers!"

Instead, what I say is: "No, not really."

She sighs and shakes her head, pacing about, her
trainers squeaking across the gym hall floor. It is
our first talent show meeting and so far, the first five

minutes have gone exactly as I predicted they would. We've established that Iris and Lucy are really good dancers, Kareen and Zoey are good enough to learn the steps, and I'm a major problem.

"You can't do any dance moves? Not one?" Lucy asks, folding her arms.

"Not that I'm aware of."

"You definitely don't have a tarantula on you right now, do you?" Zoey asks, looking me up and down warily.

"No, Zoey, I don't. Spiders aren't big dancers," I say, laughing.

No one else laughs. I stop laughing.

"Look," I continue, breaking the silence, "I know that you don't want me in your group. I tried talking to Mrs Fernley and I said to her that it wasn't fair because you'd already got your dance set up or whatever and that I didn't want to bring you down. But she wouldn't let me switch groups."

"Maybe you can ask her again," Kareen suggests. "And we can all ask her."

"Zoey and I already have." Lucy sighs. "She told us Morgan wasn't allowed to switch groups and we had to just make it work."

I try to ignore the hurt I feel at being so repulsive

to them that they already went to the teacher behind my back to get me kicked out of their group.

"We haven't even seen Morgan try the dance," Iris says, finishing her thoughtful pacing and coming to stand opposite me. "You might be able to learn it. Let's not give up quite yet. Why don't you *try* some steps?"

"Now?"

"Why not?"

"I don't think this is a good idea," I say hurriedly. "I'm really not a dancer."

"We're not expecting you to be professional level," she sighs. "Just give it a try and let's see how we go."

"In front of everyone?"

Iris glances around the empty hall. "There's no one else here."

"All of you are here," I point out.

"This is hopeless!" Lucy cries. "She can't even perform in front of us! Even if she does learn the steps, Iris, she'll have to perform them in front of an audience!"

"Come on, Morgan," Iris says in an encouraging voice. "Look, it's easy."

She takes a few steps back so she has some space.

"OK, all you have to do for the first move is step to the side, drop your shoulder and click, and then you do that again on the other side." She starts doing the move nice and slowly. "You see? Easy! You can do that, right?"

I shake my head. "I . . . I can't click my fingers."

"Are you serious?" Lucy looks at me like I'm completely mad. "You can't even click your fingers?"

No, Lucy, I can't, because if I did that move then there is a very real chance I would MUTE YOUR VOICE FOR EVER.

Iris looks as though she might burst into tears. "I've got an idea," I say. "We don't all have to do the dance."

"Yes, we do. We have to work as a stupid team, remember?" Lucy huffs.

"We have to work as a team but not necessarily on stage together," I explain. "Why don't I be in charge of lighting and sound? That way we're working as a group and you get to do your dance."

Lucy's expression brightens. The others all turn to look at Iris, the undisputed leader of the group. She's watching me carefully.

"Do you think that will be allowed? I don't want to be disqualified," she says, folding her arms.

"All Mrs Fernley said was that we have to come up with a piece that utilizes our individual talents and allows us to work together as a team. This way really ticks all the boxes. It's a great solution," I say brightly.

"Works for me!" Lucy nods.

"Great," Zoey says, moving to stand next to Iris. "We have a plan. Iris, can you show us that first move again?"

"I guess you don't need to be in this rehearsal then, Morgan," Lucy points out. "We're just going to be going through the basic steps."

"Oooh! We can go through them at Iris's sleepover tonight, too!" Kareen says excitedly.

"Yes, good idea." Zoey nods. "I'm so excited! Iris, who else is coming?"

I pick up my backpack and head out of the hall, listening to the details of Iris's sleepover that I haven't been invited to. I pull out my phone and give Dora a call, asking her to pick me up early. As I wait for her by the school gates, I feel a pang of sadness.

"Why do you look so glum?" Merlin asks, transforming from a spider into a black cat sitting at my feet.

"No reason," I reply, absent-mindedly fiddling with the pendant of my necklace.

"Is it because you have pen on your face?"

"WHAT? I have pen on my face?" I get out my phone and click on camera mode to look. There is a blue smudge across my right cheek. I lick my thumb and try to rub it off. "Brilliant. How long has that been there?"

"Since this morning."

I narrow my eyes at him. "And you didn't think it would be a good idea to tell me?"

"I thought it was much more fun to see you walk around with pen on your face all day." He sniggers, staring up at me with his bright green eyes. "So, if you didn't know about the pen on your face, what is it that you're down about?"

"Nothing," I sigh, shaking my head. "I just wish I was invited to sleepovers. Merlin, can I ask you a question?"

"Sure."

"A serious one."

"OK."

"I mean it. You can't make fun of me or say something mean. I want a *serious* witch-familiar answer."

"All right."

I take a deep breath. "Do you think I'll ever fit in at school?"

"No."

"Merlin!"

"What?" he says, licking his paw. "You asked me for a serious witch-familiar answer and I gave you one."

"You just said 'no' to me asking if I was ever going to fit in at school!"

"And?"

"And ... well ... that's not the answer you should give!"

"You mean, that's not the answer you want to hear," he corrects me. "You wanted me to say, 'Of course you'll fit in one day, Morgan, and you'll be invited to hundreds of sleepovers and people won't write mean things about you on the toilet walls.'"

"There are mean things written about me on the toilet walls? How have I missed those?"

"My job isn't to tell you what you *want* to hear. It's what you *need* to hear."

"And what I needed to hear was no, I won't ever fit in."

"That's right, and do you know why you won't ever truly fit in?"

"Why?" I huff, crossing my arms.

"Because you are a *witch*." He flicks his long tail. "And nobody at school will ever be allowed to know or understand that huge part of your life. You'll always have to hide it. You might eventually make friends, but you'll never *be* one of them or feel able to let them in. That's just the way it is, and always will be."

The week before half term, I'm sitting alone in the history classroom at lunchtime reading about William the Conqueror. Dora was a brilliant tutor but I have to admit that I wasn't much of an attentive pupil. I'd always persuade her to tell me about witch history instead of normal history. It was much more interesting, but I'm paying the price now.

"What are you doing?"

Owen comes in and sits down at the desk in front of me, swivelling in his seat to face me.

"I'm reading." I gesture to the textbook.

"Yeah, but why are you doing homework during lunch break in an empty classroom on your own?" His eyes suddenly widen in fear. "We don't have a test next lesson that I've forgotten about, do we?"

I shake my head and he breathes a sigh of relief. "No, I'm just a little behind and I've got nothing else to do so I thought I might as well do some reading."

He frowns. "I thought Iris said she was rehearsing the dance this lunchtime."

"Yeah, she is. If you're looking for her, she's in the gym hall. I think Mrs Fernley is helping the group with some of the choreography."

"I'm not looking for Iris, I just thought you were all in the same group. She told me that you're not doing the dancing, but aren't you sorting lighting? Shouldn't you be in on the rehearsal?"

"Nah, they don't really need me." I smile. "It's not that hard to flick a light switch. My lighting title is really an excuse for me to not get in their way."

Owen looks at me curiously. "Iris said that you were the one who came up with that solution. She wanted to teach you the dance moves. Have you been up to the lighting and sound box in the auditorium yet? If you wanted, you'd be able to create a very cool sequence."

"Iris is in charge, so I'll just do what she says." I look down at my book, hoping he'll get the hint and leave. Why is he rubbing it in that I can't dance?

"I'll leave you to your reading, but I was hoping I'd get the chance to speak to you today. I wanted to invite you to our party."

I snap my head up. "You . . . you're inviting me to a party?"

"Yeah." He laughs at my expression. "There's no

need to look so surprised. It's not a big deal."

"Right. Yeah. No, course. Not a big deal."

"It's going to be at Felix's house. We thought we'd—"

"Wait a second" – I hold up my hand – "you're inviting me to Felix's party? Owen, there is not a chance that he would want you to do that."

"It's *our* party, it's just being held at his house. My parents won't let me have parties at ours, so I suggested it to Felix and his parents are happy to host it."

"Oh. Well, I still don't think that Felix would want me there."

"Forget what Felix wants. It's this Saturday and it's a Halloween party. Dressing up is compulsory."

"Halloween isn't until the week after half term."

"Yeah, but isn't it more fun to celebrate during half term? That way, we celebrate Halloween *and* a whole week off school." He grins. "I'm a genius, right?"

"I'm not sure you can take credit for the idea of a Halloween party. I think it's quite a common event."

"So, are you going to join us? Come on," he says, nudging my arm when he sees me hesitating. "It will be fun."

"OK," I say quietly. "I'll come to the party."

"Great. Oh, and I already thought about what your

costume could be." He smiles mischievously. "You could dress up as a tarantula!"

"What? That's a terrible idea!"

"It's a brilliant idea. It would be you making fun of everyone else and how terrified they were on your first day."

"It would also remind everyone why they don't like me in the first place."

"Hey, that's not true. People like you," he protests.

"Oh really? Apart from you, name one person who likes me."

"Um," he says, his forehead creased in concentration. "Miss Campbell?"

"She's a teacher! And this morning she asked if I'd turned on my brain today or, in fact, any day so far this term!" I sigh. "To be fair, that's probably the nicest thing anyone in the school has said to me. The students say a lot worse."

"OK, look, it's not that people don't like you, they're just a bit scared of you, I reckon. They think a spider might jump out of your hair and bite them if they get too close."

"Thanks, that makes me feel a lot better."

"The party will change their minds. Especially if you dress up as a tarantula. Or maybe a python? There was a rumour at one point that you'd threatened Mr Hopkins with one in his office when he tried to expel you for bringing your pet spider to school. I thought that might be why he's always glaring at you and telling you off for tiny things."

"Sadly not true, but very imaginative."

"So, if you're not going to come to my awesome Halloween party as a tarantula, what are you going to dress up as?"

"I don't know. I'll have to think about it. Maybe . . . a witch?"

"Nah, don't be a witch," he says, jumping up and heading to the door as the bell rings. "That would be way too boring."

Chapter Eleven

"Boring? A boy in your class said witches were *boring*?" Mum puts her hands on her hips. "Well, I'd like to have a little word with this boy. What's his name? Maybe I'll put a hex on him and then we'll see who's boring!"

"You're on fire, dear," Dora sighs.

"Thank you, Dora. I feel on fire! On fire with empowerment!"

"No, Aggie, you're literally on fire."

Dora gestures to Mum's sleeve. She's standing close to a cluster of candles and the billowing sleeve of her blouse has consequently caught fire.

"Oh. Yes, I am." She clicks her fingers and the flames go out, the sleeve of her blouse repairing itself.

"Mum, calm down," I chuckle, leaning back on my pillows. Merlin, in the form of a warthog, is taking up all the space on the bed. "He didn't mean it in that way. He doesn't know that witches exist, remember? I think he meant that it's quite an obvious costume, that's all."

"It's the best costume!" Mum declares defiantly. "What could be better than being a witch?"

"You're supposed to be helping me think up other ideas! I need to head to the party in an hour and we haven't come up with anything."

"Whose party is this?" Mum asks, still looking annoyed at Owen's witch comment. "You haven't told us much about it yet."

"It's at this boy Felix's house, but the idea for the party was actually Ow—"

"I went to school with a boy named Felix," Dora interrupts excitedly. "He used to own a rabbit named Toast."

"That's nice," I say, sharing a smile with Mum. "I don't think this is the same Felix though."

"I wonder what happened to him," Dora sighs.

"Felix or Toast?"

"Both."

"Anyway, about the party tonight," I say, bringing the focus back to me, "any ideas for a costume?"

"Why don't you stand up, Morgan, and we can try out a few options?" Dora suggests, making herself comfortable on the end of my bed, Mac snoring in corgi form at her feet.

I get up and stand in the middle of my bedroom, so I can see myself in the full-length mirror on my wardrobe, while Dora and Mum take a good look at me with pensive expressions.

"I know!" Dora cries. "How about a marshmallow!"

She clicks her fingers and suddenly I'm encased in a giant pink marshmallow, my head sticking out of the top, my arms straight out either side, and my face painted full-on baby pink to match. My hair is sticking up towards the ceiling in two antenna-like bunches, with marshmallows stuck all the way down them.

"Dora! I can't go like this! I look ridiculous!"

"I think you look great!" she enthuses. "It's an unusual costume and very seasonal. People toast marshmallows over little Halloween bonfires!"

"I doubt I'd be able to fit into Felix's house! I'm surprised I'm even fitting into this room."

Mum giggles. "I have to agree that it's not particularly practical. How about something like this?"

She clicks her fingers and I'm suddenly wearing

jeans and a T-shirt, but I have hair EVERYWHERE. It's thick on my arms and when I see myself in the mirror I scream. I have hair, REAL hair, all over my face, growing out of my skin – and two ears poking out of my head.

"You're a werewolf! Cool, right?" Mum says smugly as I touch the hair on my face, too horrified to speak. "I met one once and they are just so polite and—"

"MUM! I CANNOT GO LIKE THIS!" I cry. "I look so WEIRD!"

"I think you make a very sweet little werewolf," Dora says. "But I suppose it does look *very* real and the other kids might not see that as a good thing."

"All right then, I have another idea," Mum says brightly, clicking her fingers and turning me into a walking clock.

After half an hour, it feels like I have tried on every Halloween costume possible, but not the cool ones that normal people wear. The really, really strange ones that my witch mother and her witch friend think up. Examples of the outrageous things I am transformed into include: a fajita, a tasselled lamp complete with a light switch, an old spell book – my head poking out of the front cover underneath the title – a dustbin, and a friendly spiky-eared goblin, modelled on the one Dora once competed with in a charity sports day for magic folk in need.

The worst one by far comes when Dora cries, "I know! How about a skeleton?" and clicks her fingers. When I look in the mirror my entire body has disappeared and I am staring at my OWN GENUINE SKELETON. I scream so loudly that our neighbour shouts out from his window, asking if he needs us to call the police.

"No thank you, Mr Mitchell! We just saw a spider and overreacted!" Mum calls back, before clicking her fingers and turning me back to normal. "Well, that was traumatizing for everyone."

"Not for me," Merlin chuckles, transforming into his black cat form and hopping up on to my desk, his tail flicking side to side. "I thought it was a major improvement."

This is the last straw.

"Let's try a—"

"ENOUGH!" I yell, interrupting Mum before she can click her fingers.

My outburst takes her and Dora by surprise and they both blink at me in shock.

"I do not want to go to this party as a pumpkin or a burrito or a giant purple blob or whatever else your bizarre brains can think up," I huff, slumping down on to the bed. "Thank you for your help, but I am going to decide on my costume myself."

Mum shares a look with Dora before she speaks. "All right then, I appreciate that our ideas probably got a bit . . . overwhelming."

"Especially when you saw your own bones," Dora adds apologetically.

"Why don't we go downstairs and give you some space to brainstorm ideas," Mum suggests, gesturing for Dora to follow her out of the room. "If you're still stuck in a bit, we can have another go."

They bustle out and I lean back on to my pillows.

"What am I going to do?" I ask Merlin. "I have to think of a cool costume. This party is my chance to show everyone I'm not a complete loser!"

"I'd love to help but I feel exhausted from having to listen to you for all my life so far." Merlin yawns. "I'm going to squeeze in a nap and you wake me up when you've solved your problems."

"Great. I couldn't ask for a better guardian," I huff sarcastically. "Where would I be without you, Merlin?"

Ignoring me, he transforms into a bat and flies up to the window, landing on the curtain rail and then hanging upside down from it, wrapping himself up in his bat wings.

I watch him and an idea pops into my brain.

"Merlin . . . you're a genius! That's it!"

He opens one wing to peer out at me as I jump to my feet and stand in front of the mirror.

"What are you talking about?"

"You've given me an idea," I say enthusiastically, staring at my reflection and preparing myself for the spell. "Without meaning to, you've actually been super helpful."

"That's disappointing," he says.

I stare hard at the mirror and, when I'm ready, click my fingers. A smile spreads across my face as I look at my reflection. I've found the winner.

"A vampire," Merlin says, soaring through the room and landing on my shoulder. "Inspired by my bat form, I take it. Not bad. I've always been a fan of vampires, ever since I heard that they're extraordinarily good at Monopoly. I suppose they have years to practise and not much else to do when they're stuck indoors during daylight hours."

I have to admit my costume is brilliant. A long, swishing black cloak with a high collar and a red silk lining hangs over my shoulders. Underneath, I'm wearing a white shirt, which has billowing sleeves and ruffles around the neck, a red and black patterned waistcoat, high-waisted black trousers and black boots. My make-up is cool too – dark eyeshadow, eyeliner with a dramatic flick, strong dark eyebrows, full fake eyelashes and deep-red lipstick. It looks like I've had it professionally done on a movie set or something.

"I'm not finished yet," I tell Merlin excitedly. "I have to concentrate for this next part."

Taking my time to really focus, I click my fingers and my hair turns jet black, then grows longer and longer before curling itself into a glossy half-up style with loose tendrils framing my face. The hair that's left down sits perfectly in gentle curls around my shoulders. Delicate diamond clips in the shape of bats are dotted all over my hair.

"Wow." Merlin examines my new hair. "That's some intricate magic you've managed there."

"And the finishing touch. . ."

I take a deep breath, nervous for how this spell is going to turn out. It's never easy to mess with your own physical features, but I know if I get it right it's going to look so *cool*.

Feeling confident and excited, I click my fingers. I grin at my reflection. It's worked.

"Fangs! Real fangs." Merlin laughs as I admire my new teeth. "I hate to compliment you, but that is great magic."

"Why, thank you Merlin. I think I'm finally ready to go to the Halloween party." I smile, my fangs glinting in the light. "Don't you?"

Chapter Twelve

"What are you supposed to be?" Felix says, looking unimpressed as he answers the door. He has gone for a Frankenstein's monster costume. "A circus freak?"

"Close!" I say, attempting to laugh it off. "I'm a vampire. I've sort of gone for a female Dracula vibe and I see you're channelling Frankenstein's monster, so technically both of us have been inspired by Gothic novels!"

Felix stares at me as though I'm an alien.

I clear my throat. "Anyway, can I come in?"

He reluctantly stands aside to let me pass. The house is bustling with people and loud music is blaring from speakers in every room.

"There you go." Felix smirks, pointing up at some

fake cobwebs dangling above my head. "That should make you feel right at home."

He pushes through the people in front of us to go into the sitting room and I stand in the hallway, not really knowing what to do. No one has acknowledged my arrival and I have no one to talk to. Iris and her friends are standing in a doorway chatting and laughing, all in the same glittery unicorn costume. They're holding cups of fruit punch.

"Go get a punch," Merlin suggests, in the form of an ant tucked under the collar of my cape. "It will probably be in the kitchen. Don't just stand here."

"Yep." I nod, wondering why I'm here at all. "Good idea. I'll go get a drink."

I make my way down the hallway, edging past clusters of people and trying not to spill any of their drinks as I squeeze through. I pause as I catch the eye of Joe, the boy I sit next to in history, and I give him a smile.

"Hey, Joe. Nice costume. Teenage Mutant Ninja Turtle, right?"

He nods, looking awkward at having to talk to me in front of his friends.

"I'm a vampire," I say enthusiastically. "You probably guessed that from the fangs."

He frowns, staring at my teeth. "Those look so ... real."

"Thanks! So, are you guys all enjoying the party?" I ask, smiling at the group.

"We *were*," one of the boys says under his breath, making the others snigger. "Are you sure Felix invited you? It seems ... unlikely."

My cheeks grow hot with embarrassment and hurt. "Owen did, actually. He—"

"Owen's in the kitchen," a girl says pointedly. "Maybe go talk to him instead."

"Right. Sorry. I'll leave you to it," I say quietly, swallowing the lump in my throat and moving on, leaving them to giggle together.

Merlin, still in his ant form, crawls up my neck and hides behind my ear so I can hear him above the music. "Permission to turn into a venomous snake and give that little friendship group a bite or two?"

"Permission not granted," I sigh, while someone barges past me as though I'm completely invisible. "I should have known better than to talk to Joe. He's made it clear in lessons that he doesn't like me."

"Well, don't be surprised if in your next history lesson, Joe gets stung on the nose by a hornet. Twice."

I manage to get to the kitchen and see Owen,

standing with a group of friends right by the stacks of cups and bowl of fruit punch. I give him a small wave to get his attention and his expression brightens on seeing me, which makes me feel a little bit better.

"Hey, Owen," I say, taking in his garish yellow costume. "Uh ... what are you? A banana?"

A smile spreads across his face. "No, I'm Pikachu. From Pokémon."

"Oh sorry. I don't really know anything about Pokémon."

"No worries." He grins. "Wow, your vampire costume is amazing. Did you dye your hair or is that a wig?"

"I dyed it. Non-permanent, but I thought it might be fun."

"It suits you!" He hesitates. "Those fangs look very real. Where did you get them?"

"A fancy-dress shop online. All the reviews were really good, so I hoped they'd turn out all right."

Owen peers at me. "It's almost as if your teeth have grown into fangs."

I laugh, reaching for a cup and pouring myself a drink. "Good one."

As I take a sip, I think I see something. A shadow flits across the ceiling. I blink and look again, but there's nothing there. Owen notices my gaze and looks over his shoulder.

"What?" he asks, turning back to me, confused. "What is it?"

"Nothing. I thought I . . . Never mind."

"You know," Felix's voice comes booming out from behind me, "some people might think it's a bit lame to dye your hair just for a party. A bit try-hard."

He appears at my side, pushing past me to help himself to the punch.

"I think it looks really cool," Owen says. "Morgan definitely wins the costume competition tonight."

"What?" Felix looks repulsed. "Because she threw on a cloak, dyed her hair and wore fake fangs? Don't be stupid, Owen. Vampire is such a boring, obvious choice for a Halloween party."

"As opposed to your costume?" Owen says, raising his eyebrows.

I laugh into my drink and Felix scowls at me.

"No one can beat Frankenstein."

"Frankenstein's *monster*." I correct him without thinking.

"What?" Felix says.

"Frankenstein is the name of the scientist in the book. You are dressed as the monster he creates." I hesitate as Felix continues to glare at me. "Not that that's important."

Owen bursts out laughing. "I guess that means you don't win the costume competition, Felix, you don't even know what you've come dressed as!"

"Like that's important," Felix mutters.

Owen continues to tease him but I'm distracted by a small, dark shadow moving quickly across the ceiling light. Then I see it, flying through the air and landing on a top shelf, hidden in the darkness.

A *bat*.

"Merlin!" I growl, narrowing my eyes at it.

"Yes?" a voice says from my collar, making me start.

"You OK, Morgan?" Owen asks, looking at me strangely.

"Yeah, yeah, I just ... uh ... I just need to go to the bathroom," I say, putting my cup down and hurrying out of the kitchen.

I get to the downstairs toilet to find Iris waiting at the door.

"There's another bathroom upstairs," she tells me, fiddling with her unicorn hairband just before the door unlocks and someone comes out.

As she heads into that one, I rush up the stairs, dodging the people standing around chatting and opening all the doors on the landing until I find the bathroom. I go in and shut the door behind me, locking it.

"Merlin, what's going on?"

"What do you mean?" he asks, transforming into a crow and going to sit on the shelf below the mirror, knocking all the soaps and bottles of lotion into the sink as he makes himself comfortable.

"Did you transform into a bat and fly around the kitchen?"

"Nope. Wasn't me."

"Are you sure?"

He tilts his head in irritation. "Yes, I'm sure."

"There's a bat in the kitchen, then. An actual bat."

"Yep. And there's also one in your cloak."

"*What?*"

I yelp loudly as a bat comes shooting out from underneath my cloak and flies into the bath, settling in the tub.

"What was a BAT doing in my cloak?" I cry, pointing at it. "How did it get in there? Is that the one from the kitchen?"

"I don't think so," Merlin says, looking at me sideways with his beady crow eye. "Because there's another one in your cloak."

I swish my cloak and another bat comes flying out, landing in the bath next to the first one.

"Merlin, WHY are there bats in my cloak? What is happening?!" I croak, trying not to panic. "Please, please, please tell me this is just a major coincidence and Felix has some kind of bat problem in his house!"

"I don't think that's what's going on here," Merlin says thoughtfully, turning into a black cat and swishing his tail. "I think it's your costume."

"What do you mean?"

"I think your costume comes with bats."

I blink at him. "How can a costume COME WITH BATS?"

I cry out in surprise as another two bats soar up from my cloak and fly around my head for a bit before landing on my shoulders.

"GET OFF, BATS!" I yell, flinging my arms around. "GET IN THE BATH WITH THE OTHERS!"

They immediately fly from my shoulders and huddle together in the bath.

"See? They listen to you," Merlin points out, chuckling. "Think about it, Morgan. You're a vampire. And vampires have an army of bats. Apparently."

As he finishes his sentence five more bats appear, flitting about the room excitedly and settling in the bath.

"I'm not an actual vampire," I seethe, staring at the cluster of bats in horror as they all stare right back at me, their master.

"I think your spell went a bit too far."

"That's an understatement!" I yell. "I am at a party with a BATHFUL OF BATS!"

Suddenly, there's a knock on the door and I freeze as I hear Owen's voice.

"Morgan? Are you in there?"

"Uh … yeah … hi … the bathroom's taken!" I call as another five bats flutter out from my cloak and begin flying around the bathroom.

I try to herd them into the bathtub but this particular gang is a little more stubborn than the previous bats. One flies straight into the toilet and starts splashing about excitedly, having a marvellous time.

"Get out of there!" I whisper, as Merlin desperately tries to stifle his laughter.

"Are you OK?" Owen continues through the door. "I wanted to check you weren't upset by anything Felix said."

"Uh n-no, I'm good! I'm great! Felix is hilarious. All fine!"

Quietly, I try to shoo the bats away from the cabinet as they manage to open it and flap their wings around the bottles, which tumble out and crash loudly into the sink. As I reach to put them all back, I knock over a glass of toothbrushes which smashes and shatters across the floor.

"Morgan? What was that? Did you just fall over in there or something?" Owen asks.

"Yes! I fell over! Ha ha, silly me!" I reply. "I'm OK though! Nothing to worry about."

A plastic bottle of shower gel has slipped from the side of the bath into the tub and is lying on its side, the gel oozing out of it. Seeing an opportunity for mischief, some of the bats start jumping up and down on the side of the bottle like it's a bat trampoline, squeaking in joy as the shower gel goes flying out, splattering across the bathroom tiles.

Other bats are busy taking it in turns to swing from the light, causing the lampshade to topple off and land on my head like a hat, just when I'm trying to gain some authority with the shower-gel bats. They all roll around laughing at me.

"What is going on in here? I heard a crashing sound."

I wince at Felix's voice as he joins Owen outside the door.

"Nothing! Everything is fine!" I call out, taking the lampshade off my head before several more bats come swishing out from my cloak and join the fun.

"You really need to take control of your bats," Merlin instructs, ducking as they fly over his head. "I have an inkling people may notice a swarm this big."

"Morgan, what's going on in there?" Owen calls, knocking again.

"It sounds like you're destroying my bathroom!" Felix yells, banging on the door as more things come crashing from the cabinet. "Open up!"

"I need the bats to all be still for a moment, so I can concentrate on a spell and get rid of them!" I whisper to Merlin as one flies right into my forehead and sends me stumbling backwards into the door.

"Yell at them!"

"I can't!" I hiss, gesturing to the bathroom door as Felix knocks again. "They'll hear me shouting instructions to bats! That will make me look really weird!"

"Morgan, I think we can safely say, whatever happens, you're going to look a bit weird." Merlin sighs, glancing around at the bathroom destruction. "Try whistling. That will get the bats' attention."

"Good idea."

I attempt to whistle but I can't do it with the stupid fangs in my mouth. I click my fingers to get rid of them, but when I lift my fingers to my mouth the fangs are still there. I look at the bathroom mirror in a panic, clicking my fingers again and again, but the fangs don't budge.

Uh-oh.

"I can't get rid of my vampire fangs! They're stuck on! What happens if I can't get my teeth back to normal? What happens if I'm stuck with fangs FOR EVER?!"

"Let's deal with one magical disaster at a time, shall we? I have an idea!" Merlin points to the bathroom window. "Open that and the bats will fly out. That solves one problem."

I fling open the window and immediately all the bats fly out happily into the night. Closing it firmly behind them, I breathe a sigh of relief.

"OPEN THIS DOOR!" Felix shouts.

I hurry over and unlock it as Merlin quickly transforms into a tiny spider and crawls up my leg. Felix's yells have obviously drawn attention as when I pull open the door with a big smile on my face, I'm faced with him, Owen and a crowd of people all waiting to see what's going on.

Felix cranes his neck to see over my shoulder and his eyes widen at the state of the bathroom.

"What happened?" he asks, more baffled than angry at this point.

"It's not as bad as it looks. It's just a few bottles that

fell out of the cabinet when I opened it looking for ... um ... make-up remover. Yeah, I put on too much eyeshadow, you know how it is. Oh, and the lampshade came off the light. I don't know how that happened. It was quite funny actually, it fell off and landed right on my head like a hat. Ha ha."

Only Owen laughs. Everyone else just stares.

"Anyway, I'll clear this up and then we can all get back to the party!"

"You are so weird," Felix says, wrinkling his nose.

Just as he turns to go back downstairs, a small bat flits up the stairs, over everyone's heads and comes in to land on my shoulder.

"Ah," Merlin whispers, having made his way up to my other shoulder, "we forgot about the one in the kitchen."

There's a split second of silence before the party descends into chaos.

"BAT! THERE'S A BAT IN THE HOUSE!" Felix screeches at the top of his voice, before screaming and running away down the stairs. Everyone else follows suit, hurrying away from me in a panic.

"I suggest you play dumb," Merlin whispers.

"ARGH, BAT!" I yell as convincingly as possible, flinging my arms around while my loyal bat friend clings on to my cloak for dear life. "There's a bat on me! Oh no!"

Someone smart throws open the front door, calling up, "Try to send it flying this way! Corner it!"

Unfortunately, it turns out that my bat army, having been tricked into flying out of the house, was patiently waiting for an opportunity to come back in. A swarm of bats comes soaring into the house as soon as the downstairs door is opened, sending screaming party guests scattering in all directions.

"Morgan!" Owen cries, still standing outside the bathroom. "That bat won't leave your shoulder!"

"Yeah! I think ... I think its claw must be caught on my cloak!"

"This is absolutely hilarious to watch!" Merlin chuckles, enjoying the chaos as I pretend to swat the bat off my cloak. "Look how terrified Felix is!"

"I have to leave," I hiss to Merlin. "They'll all follow, right?"

"It's the only way to get them out of here." Merlin sighs. "But it's a shame. We're all having so much fun."

"Morgan, wait!" Owen calls out as I hurtle down the stairs.

Luckily, there are so many people running about in terrified panic, I end up hurrying out of the front door in the middle of a bustling crowd. It's not obvious that as soon as I leave, the swarm of bats does too. I run down Felix's drive before taking cover behind a large tree on his front lawn. I crouch down as the bats come to land happily in the tree, hanging upside down from the branches.

I make sure no one is looking and then take a deep breath, feeling calmer in the cold, quiet night air.

I click my fingers and when I look up, the bats are gone. I close my eyes in relief, before reaching for my phone and calling Mum to ask her to pick me up early. I stay hidden behind the tree as the panic subsides and people head back into the house, talking about how crazy that was. After a while, I hear the music blaring out again as the party continues.

"So?" Mum asks when she pulls up. I jump into the front seat, desperate to get home. "How was it?"

"Honestly, Mum," I say with a defeated sigh, "I really, *really* don't want to talk about it."

Chapter Thirteen

There's a loud knock on my bedroom door.

"Morgan? Can we come in?"

"Yep," I call back, returning my attention to the Norman invasion factsheet I'm trying to fill out at my desk.

The door squeaks open and Mum comes in, followed by Dora. Mac is in corgi form and Helena is flitting around Mum's shoulders as a hummingbird. A mug of steaming hot chocolate topped with marshmallows floats through the air and lands next to me.

"Thanks," I say, not looking up.

"How's your homework?" Mum asks, coming to stand over me while Dora perches on my bed.

"It's OK."

"Good." She hesitates. "Morgan, can we talk to you for a moment?"

"Sure. What's up?"

"You've spent the whole half-term week shut away in your bedroom and quite frankly, we're worried about you," Mum explains, Dora nodding along in agreement. "We wondered if you wanted to talk about it."

"What happened at the party last weekend?" Dora asks gently. "You can tell us."

"Nothing happened."

They share a look before Mum says, "Something must have happened to make you so upset and we want you to know that, whatever it is, you can talk to us about it."

"I told you, the party was just really boring and then I had that little panic when I couldn't change my fangs back to normal teeth. So I decided it was time to head home." I shrug. "That's all."

"Morgan, it's OK if you—"

"She doesn't want to talk about it," Merlin says, in the form of a black cat sitting on my desk. "And trust me, that is a blessing. I've had to hear about it all week! Blah blah blah teenage problems blah blah blah."

"It's good that you've been talking about it to someone," Dora says cheerfully. "Even if that someone is Merlin."

"I haven't been talking about anything. Merlin is making things up. Nothing happened at the party. Now, I need to get back to the Norman Conquest."

"Ugh, those books are filled with lies," Dora says, nodding to my history textbook. "Nothing is ever mentioned about all the witches who healed the wounded or—"

"Because the witches had to use warlock potion to wipe the memories of those who lived to tell the stories," Mum interrupts, rolling her eyes. "Anyway, let's focus on Morgan and what's upsetting her, shall we?"

"Yes, absolutely. We are here for you, Morgan," Dora says solemnly. "Did the fangs really upset you that much? Your teeth were back to normal in just two days, which isn't so bad."

Mum nods. "I think it's wildly impressive that you did such a strong spell! For your teeth to take that long to go back to normal? It's incredible. I know you lack confidence, Morgan, but I have a feeling that you're a lot more powerful than you think." She pauses. "But I don't think it was the fangs that have been upsetting you this week. I think something else happened at the party, which you don't want to tell us about, and—"

"Look" – I put down my pen, realizing that they're not going to leave any time soon – "I'm telling you that *nothing happened*. And I'm over the fangs thing. But there is something that I do want to talk to you about."

"Go for it," Mum says, looking at me intently.

"I've been thinking about it all week and I think that I should go back to being home-schooled by Dora. You can write a letter to Mr Hopkins, Mum, and let him know that I won't be returning for the rest of the term. Trust me, he will be happy about the news."

Mum and Dora both stare at me in shock.

"But," Mum begins, "you've wanted to go to school for so long."

"Yeah, I was deluded."

"Morgan—"

"I've thought about this, Mum, and it's what I want. It turns out school isn't for me."

She nods thoughtfully and after a few moments of silence says, "Why don't we see how you feel at the end of term?"

"Mum, no, I want to leave now. I can't go back to school."

"Why not?" She raises her eyebrows. "Because of what happened at the party? You can't run away from things, Morgan."

"I'm not running away!" I cry. "I just don't want to go to school!"

"I get that school can be difficult at first," Mum says. "You've never been in that environment before and fitting into normal life is always tricky for witches. But I also think that deep down, you don't want to give up quite yet. So I'm going to offer you this compromise: you stay on at school until Christmas. If you still want to leave then, I'll speak to the headmaster and you can return to being home-schooled. If you've changed your mind and want to stay, then that's fine too. What do you think?"

I sigh, looking down at my feet. "Fine. But I'm not happy about this."

"Now, Dora and I want to take you out for some fun." She smiles warmly at me. "You've been sulking the whole week and it is *Saturday*. You should be enjoying the weekend!"

"Come on, put your shoes on," Dora chimes, clicking her fingers. My shoes fly across the room and on to my feet. "We're going pumpkin-shopping and then I'm going to teach you how to carve one like the normal human people do."

"What's the point in that?" Merlin snorts, flicking his tail.

"It's a fun activity to do all together," Dora explains, as Mac switches from a corgi into a Doberman and

141

bares his teeth at Merlin. "And sometimes clicking your fingers and getting what you want all the time can be quite boring."

As I put my seatbelt on and half-listen to Dora telling me all about the wonderful pumpkin farm she's taking us to, I consider the compromise I just made with Mum. All week I've been torn about the best decision to make. Part of me didn't want to leave my room ever again after humiliating myself at the party, let alone go to school and face everyone there. But another part of me felt a bit sad at the idea of admitting defeat and becoming a friendless witch-loser for the rest of my life.

I gaze out of the window and come to the conclusion that Mum's idea is a good one. This way, I can postpone my decision and maybe by Christmas, I'll have made progress with the whole friends thing. But it also means that I have to go to school on Monday and face everyone, and that makes me feel sick. I hope Owen isn't mad at me for ruining his party. Not that he knows it was my fault the bats were there.

But I am embarrassed about the bathroom thing. They must all think I'm such a freak for showing up to the party, throwing a load of bottles and toothbrushes around the bathroom and then disappearing without bothering to clear it up.

Why didn't I think to just click my fingers and make the bathroom perfect again before opening the door to Owen and Felix?!

I'm such an idiot, I don't deserve friends.

Maybe I can try to get Owen on his own and convince him that I'm not a total freak. But it's going to be hard to find a moment to talk to him without Felix butting in. And I don't want to embarrass him by forcing him to talk to me if he doesn't want to.

ARGH. My brain hurts with all this thinking.

As the car stops at some traffic lights, I see a lady walking down the road carrying a book bag and I have an idea.

"Dora," I say, interrupting her passionate rant about a warlock who was recently reported to be sneaking truth potions into the cups of politicians at fancy events. "Can we make a quick stop on the way to the pumpkins?"

"Of course! Whatever you like. Where do you need to go?"

I quickly try to think up a lie. I want to go to Blaze Books to speak to Owen without running the risk of all his friends being around him, but Dora will think I'm after those old witch books I'm not supposed to read.

"I need to get a toothbrush."

"A toothbrush?" Mum swivels round to give me a strange look. "We can just magic you a new one at home, Morgan."

"Yes. That's true." I nod slowly, my brain racing to think of an excuse. "But it's a very, very specific colour toothbrush that I want. I saw it in a shop and I really want that *exact* colour, and I don't know if I could describe it to you. If you just park somewhere around here, Dora, I'll run and get it. Don't worry about coming with me," I say hurriedly as I see Mum reach to undo her seatbelt, "it will be quicker if I go alone. I really want to get to that pumpkin farm!"

Once Dora finds a parking space, I leave them waiting in the car and head down the high street, turning into the deserted alley towards Blaze Books. Merlin is tucked into the pocket of my hoodie, having a snooze in dormouse form. The old bell rings above the door as I step in and Owen's dad beams at me from behind the counter.

"Ah, Morgan isn't it?" He smiles kindly at me. "How can we help? Are you after anything specific?"

"Actually, I was looking for Owen. Is he here?"

He nods, pointing to the back. "He's just sorting the English classics for me before he goes to meet his friends. Sorry if I've been holding him up."

"No, I'm not his friends ... uh ... I mean, I'm his friend, I think, but not one of those friends. Anyway, I'll go find him. Thanks."

I make my way to the back of the shop and see him crouched in the right-hand corner, reading a heavy-looking book, the stacks of English classics scattered around him untouched.

"Hey, Owen," I say quietly. His head jolts up.

"Hey, what are you doing here?" He closes his book and gets up, wiping the dust off his jeans.

"I'm on my way to go pumpkin-picking."

"Nice." He looks at me strangely. "And were you looking for a book on that?"

"No, I came here because I wanted to say sorry. For the party."

"Why?" He looks confused. "You didn't do anything."

"Well, I wanted to explain about the bathroom situation..."

"Don't worry about that. I told Felix that I heard you fall and knock the stuff over. It could have happened to anyone."

"But it was embarrassingly clumsy and I didn't manage to clear it up."

"That's OK, you were running out of the house

because a bat attacked you," he says, shaking his head. "Weird, that."

"I know. So weird that they showed up! Random. There must be some kind of bat problem in the country or something! Maybe global warming is affecting their behaviour."

"Maybe," he says, watching me with a strange expression.

"Anyway, I'll apologize to Felix about the mess when I see him."

"It was weird that the bat stuck to you," Owen says, clearly finding it difficult to get past the bat thing. "There was no shaking him off. It's like . . . he was connected to you or something."

"Yeah, that was strange. Completely coincidental and strange." I force a laugh. "And I was dressed as a vampire at the time! Maybe they mistook me for Dracula."

"The bats all flew out just after you left, by the way."

"Did they?" I ask, as innocently as possible. "Huh. What a shame. If I'd known, I would have come back to the party. They scared me so much. Right, I better go. My mum is waiting in the car and we don't want to be late for that pumpkin-picking!" I hesitate. "Sorry, again. I just wanted to make sure we were OK."

"Yeah, we're OK. Why wouldn't we be? Make sure you choose a good pumpkin," he advises as I turn to go. "I'll see you at school."

As I wander the rows of pumpkins, I think about school on Monday, and even though speaking to Owen has made me feel better about everything, I still have a sinking feeling of dread in my stomach whenever I imagine stepping through those school gates again.

"I don't get it, Morgan," Merlin says, in the form of a frog, hopping from pumpkin to pumpkin as I inspect them. "It's like you've forgotten you're a witch."

"What do you mean?" I reply, checking that no one is around to hear or see me talking to a frog.

"Just a click of your fingers and everything at school can change," he explains, tapping a webbed foot impatiently on the pumpkin. "You can be and do whatever you want."

"Are you insane? I'm not allowed to practise magic at school," I remind him, making sure Mum and Dora are out of earshot. Thankfully, they're a few rows away, arguing over what makes a pumpkin a good pumpkin. Dora is on the side of size; Mum is on the side of richness of orange colour.

"No, you *are* allowed to practise magic at school,"

Merlin corrects me. "There are no witch laws saying you can't do spells at school and many witches do them when it's safe. *You* just promised your mum you wouldn't."

"Yeah, my mum who happens to be the Great Sorceress. If I use magic and she finds out, she will KILL me."

He shrugs. "Then make sure she doesn't find out."

I stare into his innocent little frog eyes. "You think I should seriously consider this? Or is this some kind of mean Merlin trick?"

"I think it's about time you stopped being shoved around, metaphorically-speaking, by those snooty kids," he says. "Whether I like it or not, you're *my* witch. And no witch of Merlin's gets treated like a fool!"

"Wow." I raise my eyebrows at him. "Have you been watching a lot of movies recently?"

"Don't push it, Morgan," he huffs. "I'm not going to be nice for long. Just think about it. A click of your fingers and you could be the most popular kid in school, and anyone who crosses you gets what they deserve. Or," he pauses for effect, "you can continue being miserable and letting them win. Your choice."

The more I think about it, the more Merlin makes sense. I guess there would be no harm in a couple of *small* spells. Nothing fancy that might get out of hand.

Just some harmless ones that might help me to enjoy school a bit more.

Mum wouldn't have to know. Ever.

"Merlin, I think you're right." I grin, holding up the pumpkin he's sitting on. "It's time for a little bit of magic."

Chapter Fourteen

"Are you sure you want me to pull up here?" Mum asks, looking confused. "I can drop you much closer to the school if you like."

"This is good." I nod, undoing my seatbelt. "I just want a little walk up to the school. You know, get my head in the right space."

Her phone rings and she sighs as she sees it's her assistant. She presses mute.

"That's the third call this morning, and it's not even eight thirty. I am not looking forward to this Monday. Anyway, Morgan, you're not going to run away and skip school, are you? Because I would much rather you were honest with me than pretend to walk up to school and wait for me to drive off before you—"

"Mum." I hold up my hands. "I swear I'm not going to skip school. I just want a little preparation time, rather than going straight in there. OK?"

She nods. "OK."

Her phone rings again and she lifts her eyes to the ceiling.

"You should answer that and get going to work." I lean across so she can give me a kiss on the cheek and then I get out of the car, shutting the door behind me. "I'll see you tonight."

"Have a good day. Good luck," she says, before answering the call and pulling away down the road.

I wait until her car has turned the corner, then dash across the road and into an old red telephone box. The windows are cloudy, like they haven't been cleaned in a while, making it difficult to see in or out.

"OK," Merlin says, in tarantula form on my shoulder. "Let's start with the witch backpack."

I get my phone out and bring up a recent search I did on some new designer bags, clicking on my favourite one – a bag that I saw Iris showing her friends on her phone a couple of weeks ago, saying how much she wanted it.

"Very nice," Merlin says, nodding in approval. "What colour are you going to get it in?"

"Black!" I laugh. "Duh, I'm a witch."

I focus on the bag onscreen before clicking my fingers. My backpack transforms into the coolest black bag I have ever seen.

"I love it," I squeal, clutching it to me. "SO much better than the backpack. Wait until Iris sees this!"

"OK, now what about your shoes?"

"What about my shoes?"

Merlin scuttles forward to point one of his many legs accusingly at my feet. "Those shoes are bringing you down. Do you think a witch should be wearing those clunky, ugly clog-wannabes? *Do you?*"

"I have to stay within the uniform guidelines."

"Which are?"

"Something like 'sensible black shoes'."

"Do you know what are, technically, sensible black shoes?" Merlin says in a mischievous voice. "Doc Martens. They would suit you and look good. Go on, try them and see how it looks."

I focus, click my fingers and look down at my feet to see a brand-new pair of Doc Martens. This is FUN. With Merlin's guidance, I add some wayfarers to my look, along with a delicate gold bracelet with blue stones that matches the pendant Mum gave me. Merlin points out that my hair could do with a brush, so I click my fingers and it looks like I've just had it professionally styled.

"I think you're ready to go to school now," Merlin announces. "And I promise to stay hidden this time. Let's go."

I open the door of the telephone box and walk a few paces until Merlin shouts "STOP" in my ear and orders me to go back into it.

"What's wrong?" I ask in a panic, wondering if my spells have already messed up.

He sighs, shaking his head, and crawls down my arm so that he can stand on my hand and address me properly.

"It's your walk."

"What about it?"

"It's RUBBISH."

"My walk is rubbish? But Merlin, that's how I walk."

"If you want these people to respect you, you have to show them that you respect yourself! I'm on your shoulder and you're so hunched over, I'm practically walking on the ground. And I was very tempted just then to reach out one of my legs and tickle your chin, because it was almost touching your neck."

I roll my eyes. "OK, firstly, you're exaggerating, and secondly, you are not a military commander. I can walk however I want." I pause for a few moments before quietly asking, "Is it really that bad?"

"Yes. When you walk, you remind me of that zombie we had round for Sunday roast."

"What? Merlin, we've never had a zombie round for Sunday roast!"

"Really? Oh. That must have been a previous life. Anyway, it's not difficult. You have to pretend to be a really confident witch. If you think that, you'll naturally become one. As you walk, think to yourself, 'I am a cool, brilliant witch. And you lot are losers!' or something along those lines."

I can't believe what I'm hearing. I stare at him, smiling dopily.

"Why are you looking at me like that?" he asks. "Stop it. You look happy and it's very unpleasant."

"Why can't you give me this lovely advice all the time? This is a side to you I have never seen and I feel that—"

"PLEASE don't talk to me about your *feelings*. Bleugh!" He scuttles up my arm and tucks himself under my collar. "Let's get moving before more hair starts sprouting on your face and we die of old age."

"What do you mean *more* hair?!"

"Come on!" he says as the bell rings in the distance. "You're going to be late."

I race to the school, clutching my new bag, trying not to trip over my new shoes and thinking, "I am a cool, brilliant witch" over and over. As I walk up the steps to the doors of the building, I make sure my sunglasses are in place and take a deep breath.

"Here we go," whispers Merlin.

The reaction to my entrance could not have been better. As I walk down the corridor, keeping my sunglasses on long enough for people to notice, heads start turning in my direction. I take the sunglasses off and swish my glossy hair. I see Iris do a double take and then her jaw drops when she notices the bag on my shoulder. Standing next to her, Felix looks stunned when he turns to see what she's staring at and then a bit annoyed. I smile to myself as I approach my locker.

If I was in a movie right now, this bit would totally be in slow motion and set to an AWESOME soundtrack.

I'm just thinking about which hype track would be most appropriate for my entrance, when I walk straight into Mr Hopkins, causing me to stumble backwards and almost lose my balance. I hear a loud "HA!" from Felix behind me.

So much for the cool slo-mo scene. Still. It was a nice few seconds.

"Morgan Charmley!" Mr Hopkins thunders, towering over me. "Why can't you watch where you're going?"

I am a cool, brilliant witch. I am a cool, brilliant witch.

"Sorry, Mr Hopkins," I say calmly. "It won't happen again. How was your half term?"

He looks taken aback by my reaction, but instead of answering my question, he barks, "DETENTION! After school."

"What? That seems a bit—"

"Don't argue back, or you'll be getting detention for the rest of the term!" He purses his lips. "Do NOT be late for assembly."

With that, he storms off down the corridor, muttering about misbehaving students. Owen, who was standing nearby, comes over to me.

"That was weird. Detention for bumping into him in a corridor? He really has it in for you."

"Yeah," I say, watching Mr Hopkins' back as he saunters off. "Ever since day one."

"You heading to assembly?" Owen asks. I nod and fall into step with him. "Nice boots, by the way."

I muse over Owen's question about why Mr Hopkins dislikes me so much and what happened on that first day to make me his least favourite pupil. I knew that the tarantula incident had caused a LOT of problems. Some parents had written him angry letters and others had even demanded an inspection of the school by a pest control company, which had meant closing the building down for a couple of days.

But, I remind myself, he seems to *resent* me for seeing him salsa dance. Which is very unfair. It wasn't my fault that he was practising his dance moves during the school day and, if anything, he should be GRATEFUL that I haven't told a single person about his secret. Surely, that should put me in his good books. A trustworthy, non-judgemental student.

That's not how he treats me, though. Any time I see him, he makes it very clear that he doesn't want me at school here.

And that's because I know his secret. But if everyone knew about his salsa dancing, he wouldn't resent *me* any more, because *everyone* would know. The problem would be solved. Right?

Hmmmmmm. *Mwahahahahahaha.*

Mr Hopkins steps up on to the stage once we've all sat down and everyone falls silent.

"Welcome back, students and teachers. I trust you all had a good half term and you are now feeling refreshed and ready to tackle the weeks up to Christmas. Just a few notices to give you this morning before you hurry off enthusiastically to your lessons. Firstly, big congratulations to our Year Nine first netball squad who won their match on the last day before half term and are now through to the next round of the nationals! Well done!"

He leads a round of applause and I know that this is my chance. I bend forwards pretending to fiddle with my shoe, focus and click my fingers. Nobody hears it over their clapping. I sit up and then I wait.

"My next notice is regarding. . ."

He hesitates, glancing down at his feet. I crane my neck over the heads in front of me and smile to myself as I spot one of his feet tapping a rhythm.

He clears his throat. "As I was saying, my next announcement is regarding the school talent show. I'm thrilled to see so many—"

One of his legs suddenly kicks out, his toe pointed.

There's a collective gasp. I am desperately trying not to laugh.

"S-sorry," he says, looking flustered, "I ... I don't know what just happened there, a muscle spasm. Anyway, I—"

He throws the pieces of paper he's holding up

into the air and spins on the spot. Suddenly, his hips start swaying and, when they do, he lets out a yelp of horror.

The auditorium erupts with uncontrollable laughter. The other teachers look on, stunned, most of them clapping their hands to their mouths as they try not to point and laugh at their boss. The students are having a wonderful time, some up on their feet calling for Mr Hopkins to show more of his dance moves.

"I think," Merlin whispers gleefully in my ear, "a little music wouldn't go amiss."

"I couldn't agree more."

I click my fingers and salsa music fills the auditorium. Mr Hopkins lurches forwards to take the hands of the teacher nearest to him, Miss Campbell, and drags her to her feet, twirling her across the stage.

"I'M SO SORRY, MISS CAMPBELL! I'M SO SORRY!" he squeals as he launches into a slick salsa routine, spinning her about so fast she looks as though she's going to topple over from dizziness. "I CAN'T SEEM TO STOP! I CAN'T STOP SALSA DANCING!"

Students quickly hold up their phones to film their headmaster, some of them laughing so hard that tears are rolling down their cheeks. I smile triumphantly, watching this wonderful spectacle unfold before my eyes.

I stealthily hold a finger up to my collar and a tarantula's leg protrudes to give me a mini high-five.

Justice is served.

Chapter Fifteen

"Settle down, everyone," Miss Campbell cries, waving her arms around, desperately attempting to get our attention. "Class! Please! Settle down!"

It took a LONG time for the teachers to gain control of the situation in assembly and get us off to our classrooms for the first lesson. Mr Hopkins continued salsa dancing for another few minutes before he pranced out of the hall and back to his office. Now that we've finally been herded to our lessons, no one can stop talking about his stunning performance.

"Did you see his hips?" Felix cries, jumping up on to his chair and doing an impression, making everyone laugh. "Who knew our headmaster had so much rhythm?"

"All right, Felix, that's enough!" Miss Campbell yells, rapping her knuckles on her desk. "PLEASE, everyone, SIT DOWN!"

I sit quietly next to Joe, who is ignoring me as usual and chatting excitedly about the assembly with the two boys sitting at the desk in front of us. Calmly opening my history textbook, I smile to myself in the knowledge that Mr Hopkins got what he deserved and I am now off the hook. Hopefully, after salsa dancing around the school all day, he'll be so distracted that he'll forget about the detention he gave me.

"Nice dancing yourself, Miss Campbell," Felix calls out, winking to the rest of the class.

"Thank you, Felix. It was rather unexpected," she says, patting her hair nervously, "but quite a fun way to start the day. It's nice to know that Mr Hopkins has an interesting hobby outside of his school life. I think it was a unique method from the headmaster to inspire you all into livelier spirits. Let's tackle the Norman Conquest in the same way that Mr Hopkins tackled the assembly: with gusto!"

Everyone groans.

"Miss Campbell, you can't really expect us to sit here and have a normal lesson after that assembly." Felix laughs. "We just saw you and our headmaster salsa dancing!"

"Before today, I thought Mr Hopkins was intimidating." Iris shrugs. "Now, not so much."

"Yeah, whenever he tries to give me detention, I'm just going to do this." Felix stands up, poses with his hands in the air and then begins to sway his hips along the rows of desks, egged on by the rest of the class clapping him along.

He stops suddenly in front of my desk, his eyes resting on the bag at my feet.

"Oh yeah, that reminds me. What happened to the broomstick backpack, Charmley?" He sneers. "Good effort at trying to fit in, but you'll always be a loser to me."

There are sniggers from the rest of the class.

"Felix, if you don't sit down in the next three seconds, I'm going to give you detention for the rest of the week. I mean it," Miss Campbell threatens.

Still smirking at me, he backs away and then saunters to his desk.

"If you don't teach that guy a lesson," Merlin whispers from under my collar, "I'm going to."

"Don't worry, I'll handle it," I mumble.

"Who are you talking to?" Joe asks, giving me a strange look.

"Oh, just the tarantula on my shoulder." I smile innocently, turning to him.

His eyes grow wide. "You're ... you're kidding, right?"

"Sure."

We both turn our attention back to the front of the classroom where Miss Campbell is writing on the board, but I notice him shuffle his chair even further away from me.

It's difficult to concentrate on the Norman Conquest when you're plotting revenge on your nemesis. The thing is, I've never done anything to Felix to justify the way he treats me. And it's not just me. I've witnessed him making snide comments about other students, like when he makes fun of Jenny in P.E. Yeah, she's not my biggest fan because I accidentally insulted her, but she is also a nice person as far as I can tell and probably the smartest girl in our class. She's always getting the top marks. Who cares that she's not sporty? Why should that bother Felix?

It's time he got a taste of his own medicine.

And I know just what to do. His reaction to Merlin as a tarantula on the very first day revealed that he wasn't a fan of spiders, and he explained the reason a few days later when I overheard him talking to Owen.

"It's the legs," he had said, pretending to retch. "Bugs creep me out. And the bugs with a lot of legs are the worst. Why do they need to exist? Can't we just blast them all away or something? How come someone hasn't invented something to do that yet?"

At the time, I'd shaken my head at his ignorance, but now I'm delighted that he's given me the perfect ammo to secure my vengeance.

The bugs with a lot of legs are the worst.

I wait until a good moment and when Miss Campbell asks us all to turn to page seventy-three in our textbooks, the general murmur and the sound of everyone getting their books out from their bags and flicking through the pages provides me with the perfect cover.

I click my fingers under my desk.

There's suddenly a loud scream from Felix and he jumps to his feet. He's in such a hurry to get away that he stumbles, sending his chair flying backwards and then falling over the chair legs on to the floor.

"HELP!" he screams, his right arm flailing as he scrambles across the floor. "GET IT OFF! GET IT OFF ME!"

"Felix!" Miss Campbell gasps. "What on earth are you—"

"GIANT CENTIPEDE! GIANT CENTIPEDE!" he shrieks at the top of his lungs. "ON MY ARM!"

Grinning from ear to ear, I quickly click my fingers

again as the whole class jumps up to look at him and Miss Campbell comes rushing forwards.

She stands over him and sighs, angrily crossing her arms as he lies sprawled across the floor, continually whimpering, his eyes shut.

"Felix. Are you referring to that tiny ladybird on your arm?"

He opens one eye and looks down, where a little red ladybird is sitting on his elbow.

"It ... it was a ... I'm telling you ... a centipede ... it was there ... giant ... the size of my forearm ... the legs ... so many legs. . ." he wheezes, shaking his head in disbelief.

The class begins sniggering and Miss Campbell orders everyone back to their seats. Owen helps Felix up to his feet. He's brushing himself down, glancing nervously over his shoulder and spinning on the spot to make sure there's no centipede on him.

"I'm telling you. . . Owen, did you see it?"

Owen shakes his head. "All I can see is a ladybird."

"B-but it was there. So many legs. It had so many legs."

"Felix, you are on your last warning," Miss Campbell seethes. "I'm fed up of you disrupting my lesson for attention. Now, *sit down.*"

"Miss Campbell, I swear," he says, examining the floor around him. "I swear it was a centipede. I saw it."

"Well, you've certainly proven your acting skills. Save it for the talent show." She turns back to the board. "Sit down, Felix, or you're getting detention."

As he wobbles his way back to his desk, I wait until he's about to sit down and then I click my fingers. His chair slides backwards and he falls to the floor with a loud thud. The class erupts into raucous laughter.

"FELIX!" Miss Campbell shouts.

"The chair moved! That wasn't my fault!" he insists as Owen, chuckling away next to him, holds his chair for him to sit down in.

"Owen, did you move his chair?" Miss Campbell huffs, folding her arms.

He holds up his hands. "I swear I didn't. But it was hilarious. I wish I could take credit."

Giving Felix a VERY stern look, Miss Campbell returns to her scribbles on the board. I giggle as I hear Felix whispering to Owen, *The chair moved. I swear!*

I leave Felix in peace, thinking that he's probably had enough of a fright to lay low for the rest of the lesson, but he proves me wrong. After ten minutes, he's laughing at himself and his overreaction, wondering how he hallucinated a centipede on his arm and blaming it on all the horror movies he watched over half term. Slowly and surely, he goes back to his normal self and when Miss Campbell asks Jenny a question and then praises her answer, Felix can't resist a jibe.

"Nerd," he says under his breath, but loud enough for Jenny to hear.

As those around him snicker, Jenny slides down in her seat. I narrow my eyes at the back of Felix's head, trying to work out what to do next.

"Morgan?" Miss Campbell says, jolting me from my scheming. "Would you care to answer?"

"Uh, sorry, what was the question?"

She gives me a stern look and then repeats herself. "I asked you to name a mistake that the Saxons made at the Battle of Hastings."

"Right. Cool."

"Can you name one?"

"Yes. Of course! I can absolutely name one." I pretend to cough and as I do, I click my fingers. An answer writes itself in ink across the lines of my notepad, open in front of me. "Uh, the Saxons had the advantage of being uphill where they created a wall of shields. So, the Normans pretended to retreat and that was when the Saxons made the mistake of following them, breaking the shield wall and losing their hill advantage."

Miss Campbell breaks into a wide smile. "VERY good, Morgan! What an excellent answer."

I sit up a little taller as she turns back to the board. It's a really nice feeling when you get the answer right.

Felix covers his mouth with his hands, pretending to cough as he says, "Wannabe nerd." He picks up his pen and starts writing notes, looking very pleased with himself.

I remember Owen telling me about the time Felix wet himself when they were in junior school and decide that now seems like a good moment for Felix to relive that experience.

Miss Campbell, also growing tired of Felix's nonsense, gives me the best possible opportunity when she asks him to come up to the board and copy out some bullet points.

"Are you sure you don't want *Jenny* to do it?" he groans.

"I'm quite sure, thank you. Get up here."

"Fine," he sighs, standing up and ambling to the front, smirking at Jenny as he passes her. She keeps her head down, her nose almost touching her piece of paper.

Always thrilled to be given a chance to show off, Felix takes the pen from Miss Campbell and launches into a salsa dance move, making her jump and the rest of the class laugh. Grinning at how hilarious he is, he turns to the board and starts writing.

I click my fingers.

A small wet patch appears on Felix's trousers and begins to spread across his bottom. Jenny is the first to spot it, gasping loudly. Soon the rest of the class notices and everyone begins to glance at each other in disbelief before the giggles begin.

"What?" Felix frowns, spinning round to see everyone staring and laughing at him. "What is it? Did Owen stick something on my back?"

Miss Campbell turns to look at what everyone is making a fuss about.

"Oh," she says, flustered. "Um, Felix, let's pop outside, shall we?"

It's at this moment that he looks down and sees it running down his leg. He snaps his head back up to face the class.

"I haven't... This isn't... I don't know what's going on b-but..." he stammers, clutching the sides of his trousers in a panic.

"It's OK, it happens," Miss Campbell says gently, guiding him out. "Everyone else, back to work!"

"NO! No! This wasn't me!" he cries out, addressing the class as she ushers him to the door. "I don't want them all thinking... I don't know what's happened! I haven't wet myself!"

This sets off a fresh eruption of giggles and Felix continues to protest his innocence as he's led out of the room. We hear, "I SWEAR! I HAVEN'T WET MYSELF!" echoing all the way down the corridor and I feel pleased with the knowledge that Felix's little incident will be all over the school by morning break.

As I lean back in my chair to enjoy the reaction to my genius magical revenge on the school bully, I notice that Owen isn't laughing along with everyone else.

He's sitting alone, watching me intently from across the room.

Chapter Sixteen

"You know, I'm really starting to enjoy school," Merlin remarks later on in the week, in the form of a bat hanging upside down from my bedroom curtain rail. Since the Halloween party, it's been his favourite form to take. "Watching Felix checking his trousers every five seconds in case of a repeat accident is extremely entertaining."

I peer at him over my book. "Yeah, I guess."

"That wasn't very enthusiastic." He snorts. "I thought you'd be happy. Since Monday, Felix has been skulking about the school and has barely said a word to you. He knows he doesn't really have the right to make fun of anyone else now. And Mr Hopkins hasn't told you off or given you a single detention!"

"I haven't seen Mr Hopkins. He's been keeping to his office. Rumour has it, he's still salsa dancing."

"Huh." Merlin pauses. "I thought you cast a spell for him to salsa just for a day."

"So did I."

"Oh well, I'm sure it will wear off soon and at least it keeps him out of your hair."

"And for that, I am very grateful."

"So what is it? Why the ugly sad face?"

"The expression is 'why the long face?'," I correct.

"I know that. I was just being factually accurate."

I narrow my eyes at him and he cackles.

"Come on, talk to me." He opens his wings and wiggles his two little claws. "What's troubling you? I can see that something's on your mind."

I put down my book. "All right then. I think it's great that Felix has backed off and I couldn't be happier that I haven't seen Mr Hopkins all week, but I still haven't got any closer to what I actually want."

"And that is?"

I shrug. "Having friends. That's why I've always wanted to go to school. Iris still hasn't commented on my bag, even though I'm certain it's the one she wants."

"Let me get this straight," Merlin begins, "you

think that because you have a cool bag, Iris should immediately want to be friends with you?"

"I'm not an idiot," I say, rolling my eyes. "But I thought she'd at least come up and talk to me about the bag and then maybe I could—"

"Win her over with your wit and charm?" He folds his wings around himself. "Why don't you just start talking to *her*? She doesn't seem as bad as the others."

"Be serious, Merlin." I plump up my pillows and lie back, staring up at the ceiling. "If only there was a magic spell to make instant friends."

"There may not be one of those, but I think there is a way of getting in with Iris and those girls."

He drops off the curtain rail and soars across the bedroom to land on my forehead.

"Argh, get your bat feet off my face! Why do you always have to land on my head?"

"The talent show," he states simply, hopping on to the pillow and transforming into a black cat so he can curl up next to me.

"What about it?"

"Iris cares about it. A lot. So if you help her to win, she'll love you! Easy. You'd be the most popular girl in school."

"Yeah, super easy," I scoff. "I can't just click my

fingers and get her to win! She wouldn't even know that she had won because of me! What would be the point?"

"That's not what I'm thinking," he says in a tired voice. "What if your contribution made your group win?"

"Obviously that would work," I say slowly, trying to figure out what he's getting at. "But do you really think that a good lighting sequence and soundtrack would help our group win?"

"No." He gives me a wide cat grin. "But a professional dancer might."

"Everyone grab a mat and find a space," Mrs Fernley instructs, clapping her hands. "We'll start with a really fun warm-up and then we're going to try some basic gymnastics moves. Let me see that energy!"

I make sure I'm one of the first to the mats and then I move right into the middle of the room. Usually, I'd reluctantly pull one of the last mats left to the very back corner of the class, but I'm feeling confident today. Iris's mat is right next to mine and she looks confused that I've positioned mine so centrally.

"Hey, how's the dance routine coming along by the way?" I ask her while everyone else is getting their mat sorted. "Do you need me to come to any rehearsals yet?"

She shakes her head. "No, that's all right. I think you'd just be really bored."

"I was wondering whether the offer still stands for me to join in on the actual dancing," I say casually, stretching my arms over my head.

With an amused smile, she puts her hands on her hips. "Now? We've only got a few weeks until the talent show!"

"Plenty of time for me to pick it up."

"But you wouldn't even *try* last time and that was when you had a whole term left to work on it," she points out.

"I've been practising."

She raises her eyebrows. "You've been practising dancing?"

"Yep. And I've surprised myself with how much I've come along."

Lucy pulls her mat up and drops it next to mine, looking annoyed that I'm next to Iris. Felix has taken Iris's other side and, I'm sure, is listening in to our conversation. His lack of commentary so far proves that the wetting-himself thing really got to him and he's being a lot more cautious.

Yesterday, when he made a mean comment about Jenny's fringe, she looked straight into his eyes and went,

"At least I'm not still wetting myself at thirteen years old, Felix," and just swanned right on past him.

It was magical to watch.

"What are you two talking about?" Lucy asks, intrigued that Iris has bothered chatting to me for this long.

"Morgan wants to learn the dance for the talent show."

"You're kidding, right?" Lucy looks me up and down. "You can't dance."

"She's been practising," Iris explains.

"So? You couldn't even handle clicking your fingers and stepping in time before. I highly doubt that you can pick up the complex moves of our routine," Lucy says, checking her ponytail is in place.

"Clicking my fingers like this?" I say, demonstrating.

"Yes, genius," Felix interjects, unable to hold back any longer. "Well done, you've worked out how to click your fingers. I don't think that qualifies you to join a dance routine for the talent show."

"Exactly." Lucy nods smugly. "You need to stick to lighting. Sorry."

"OK." I shrug. "It's your decision. Maybe I'll ask Mrs Fernley if I can join another group who are doing a dance routine, since you don't want me to join yours."

"I don't think there will be many takers," Felix says.

"If you say so, Felix." I smile.

Out of the corner of my eye I see him share a confused look with Lucy and then Mrs Fernley starts leading the warm-up, turning on some music that fills the hall.

"Great stuff!" Mrs Fernley calls out enthusiastically. "Step side to side everyone, side to side. Get those limbs moving! That's it! Very good!"

As I listen to the music, I can feel something happening all the way through my body. I cast the spell when I clicked my fingers during our conversation, but I'm waiting for the perfect moment to test out how well it worked.

"Fantastic!" Mrs Fernley smiles, whooping to the music as the warm-up gets more energetic. "Now, let's add a little jump to our side-to-sides. That's it. A small hop! Wonderful!"

As I step to my right and jump, suddenly I spin in the air and land with some amazingly quick footwork. Lucy and Iris immediately stop what they're doing and stare at me open-mouthed.

"What ... what just..." Lucy begins, but her words fizzle out.

"What's going on in the middle there?" Mrs Fernley

calls from the front, making everyone turn to look. "Come on! I want to see you moving!"

The spell kicks in and the music changes to a hip-hop song, turning up to full volume. I launch into an amazing dance routine. The magic takes over me and I have no control over my limbs any more. My feet are crossing and spinning me around, my hips are twirling and jolting, and my shoulders are popping all over the place. I'm moving so fast, I can't really see anyone's reactions, but everyone in the class gathers into a circle around my mat and after a few seconds they begin to cheer and clap along.

Feeling like it's time to stop, even though I don't want to, I do a tiny run up along my mat and finish with a backwards somersault.

My audience bursts into applause and as Mrs Fernley turns off the music, her jaw on the floor, I'm bombarded by questions and compliments.

"Oh my god! That was AMAZING!"; "How did you do that?"; "Morgan, where did you learn those moves?"; "Can you teach us?"; "That was the coolest dance EVER!"; "Are you secretly on the West End?"; "Where did that come from?"; "Morgan, you were awesome!"

I smile at everyone, catching my breath, grateful that

they're all talking over each other so I can get away with not actually answering any of the questions.

"Morgan," Iris says, looking at me in awe, "that was *incredible*. Where did you learn to dance like that? How is this even possible? You looked like you should be in a music video!"

"Oh my god, Morgan, I take back what I said before, I am SO sorry," Lucy gushes, grabbing my arm and smiling broadly up at me. "Will you PLEASE be a part of our dance act for the talent show? Please, please, please?"

"All right. If you want."

"YES!" Lucy punches the air. "We're going to WIN! Now, seriously, HOW did you become that good at dancing in just a few weeks?"

Iris nods. "You must have been practising so much! It's amazing."

"I know what's happened here," Lucy says suddenly, looking at me suspiciously before addressing the rest of the class. "I think Morgan was always this good at dancing and has been playing a joke on us!"

They all turn to look at me in anticipation.

"Yep." I nod slowly. "Yes, that makes a lot of sense. I was just joking before. Ha ha. Pretending to be really bad."

Lucy bursts out laughing. "You pretended to be SO bad! You know, we should have guessed. No one could be *that* bad at dancing."

"Can we get on with the lesson now?" Felix yells. "I'm bored."

Mrs Fernley, who up until this point has been as intrigued as everyone else, suddenly realizes that she's supposed to be leading a lesson and clears her throat.

"Uh, yes, yes, everyone back to their mats!" she calls out, before addressing Iris. "It looks like your group will need to change up your routine for the talent show. Morgan will be taking centre stage!"

Iris's face falls slightly.

"I'm happy to do whatever you tell me to," I say quickly, not wanting her to hate me for a new reason. "You should continue leading the group."

"Don't be silly, you're an incredible dancer," she replies, collecting herself and giving me a weak smile. "Who knew?"

Chapter Seventeen

"Morgan! Sit with us!"

I blink stupidly at Lucy, who is waving for me to join her at the lunch table she always sits at with Iris, Felix, Owen and the other popular students from our year. I glance behind me to check that there's not another Morgan standing behind me.

"Come on!" Lucy smiles warmly, gesturing to the space opposite her, next to Iris.

I slowly walk over and sit down, placing my tray on the table. I can't believe this is happening. I'm sitting with a group of people at lunch in the canteen. I have friends to sit with. Actual friends!

"What a great rehearsal yesterday," Lucy says, picking up her fork and stabbing at a piece of broccoli, before addressing the others at the table. "Morgan has been adding the coolest moves into our routine over the last few days. Wait until you all see it!"

There's a murmur of excitement around the table. I keep my head down, focusing on sipping my water and hoping no one asks me any questions. Since my dance outburst in that P.E. lesson, we've had several talent-show rehearsals after school and I've had to dodge a hundred questions from the girls about where, when and how I learned to dance like I do. I can't believe I've got away with it. Not that I should be surprised; it's not like anyone would jump to the conclusion that I must be a witch.

It's nice being noticed for a good reason. Lucy and Iris have started smiling at me when I pass them in the corridors and even Joe doesn't recoil in his normal manner when I sit down next to him. He keeps asking me if I can teach him how to do the running man.

And now here I am at a lunch table, having been invited to sit here by my new *friends*. It's an amazing feeling. I don't know why I didn't use magic to make things easier for myself sooner.

"Have I told you what our group is doing for the Christmas talent show, Morgan?" Owen asks, stealing a chip from Iris's plate.

I shake my head. "I don't think so."

"It's hilarious," Iris informs me. "Owen is in a group with Jenny, and one of her many hidden talents is magic."

I drop my fork and it clatters loudly on my plate. I quickly pick it up again. "Sorry, what were you saying?"

"Magic tricks," Owen explains. "She's teaching our group and I have to say, some of the tricks are really cool."

Felix snorts. "Magic is so lame."

"No, it's not." Owen smiles, throwing a chip at him. "Wait until you see some of the card tricks I'll be doing up on that stage. Your mind will be blown, Felix."

"I don't think so. I bet you anything that I'll be able to explain every single trick you do," Felix claims, causing Iris to roll her eyes. "It's all about illusion, right? Making people look one way while you trick them, or using a fake card pack that's set up. Magic is stupid."

For a moment, I think Owen's eyes flicker to me. But when I glance at him quickly, he's looking down at his plate. I shake my head, amused at my own paranoia.

"I don't know," Owen says. "I think magic is pretty cool, when it's done in the right way."

"Magic tricks are better than your group's entry,"

Lucy says to Felix playfully. "You're just going to stand up there with a toy."

Felix narrows his eyes at her. "Yo-yos are NOT a toy."

He reaches into his pocket and gets out a red yo-yo, before showing us some tricks with it to prove his point.

"You won't be laughing when you see our synchronized routine," he continues. "It will be much better and much more interesting than whatever dance routine you lot have come up with."

"You can say whatever you like," Iris says with a giggle, "but it's still just a toy on a bit of string."

As Lucy laughs, she accidentally knocks her glass, spilling water all over her tray. It splashes on her and she jumps to her feet, making sure that it doesn't go over her school skirt. I hand her some napkins.

"Thanks, Morgan," she says, dabbing at the droplets on her skirt. "That was lucky. I almost had a little accident like Felix."

Felix scowls at her, blushing furiously. Her comment prompts plenty of sniggers from the tables around us as well as our own.

"*I told you*," he hisses, "a glass of water must have spilled on me somehow! For the last time" – he raises his voice so everyone can hear – "I did not wet myself!"

"But there wasn't a glass of water anywhere near you," I point out with a sly smile.

If Felix doesn't like his friends poking fun at him, he absolutely hates any taunts coming from me. He looks as though he might explode with anger and even Owen looks surprised at my input.

"I did not wet myself," he repeats through gritted teeth, glaring at me. "And hey, even if I did, at least people still want to hang out with me. Unlike you, Charmley. You may be able to dance, but everyone still thinks you're a *freak*."

He starts playing with his yo-yo again, a satisfied smile creeping across his face.

Silence descends upon our table. Iris shifts in her seat uncomfortably and Lucy purses her lips, unable to look at me. Owen looks frustrated, as though he's trying to search for the words but he's not sure what's best to say.

As I watch Felix show off his yo-yo tricks with that stupid smug smile on his face, the rage bubbles up inside me. I remember that when the bat landed on my shoulder at his party, he didn't look all that smug or powerful. He screamed and ran away. Maybe if he remembered how it felt to be powerless, he'd be knocked down a few pegs. I lower my hand under the table and click my fingers.

There's a strange fluttering sound from outside the canteen.

Suddenly, a swarm of bats comes flying through the window and into the room, diving straight at our table.

The canteen descends into chaos as all the students start screaming and stampeding through the doors, out into the corridor. Lucy shrieks in horror and then dives under the table with Iris and Owen to take cover as the bats come flying right at us.

Felix falls off his chair and then scrambles to his feet to try to run away, but his yo-yo unravels and the string wraps itself around his legs, causing him to trip up. The bats ignore everyone else and flutter around him as he tries to wave them off. He manages to free his legs from the string then gets to his feet, running out of the canteen with the bats in hot pursuit.

"A-are they gone?" Iris asks, peeking her head out from under the table.

"They're gone," I assure her, calmly standing up from my chair. "Are you all right?"

"QUICK!" Joe yells from the corridor. "Felix is being chased around the school yard by a swarm of bats! They won't leave him alone!"

The students still in the canteen emerge from their

hiding places and head out into the corridor and down to the front of the school building, I imagine to watch Felix run about screaming hysterically, unable to shake the swarm.

"An army of bats?" A voice sniggers on my shoulder.

"What can I say, Merlin?" I smile, putting my tray away and skipping out of the empty room. "I missed the little critters!"

I reach into my locker to get my books for the next lesson, watching in amusement as a group of students rush past me towards the front doors.

"He's being chased by bats? Are you sure?" one of them asks in disbelief.

"Yep! Apparently they got into the canteen. Just like what happened at his party!" another squeals. "They must like his smell or something; he's the only person they're chasing."

Mr Hopkins appears around the corner, his hips swaying.

"Don't run in the corridors!" he yells after them.

One of them looks back over her shoulder and sniggers.

"But we're allowed to salsa dance down them?" she calls out, before continuing to run towards the doors and flinging them open, the whole group laughing their heads off.

"*Why can't I stop dancing?*" Mr Hopkins seethes, not even noticing me as he rushes past. "And why are there BATS in my school?! This is most definitely not my year."

Smiling to myself, I shut my locker.

"Hey, Morgan."

I yelp, jumping out of my skin. Owen is leaning on the locker next to mine.

"How long have you been standing there?" I ask, clutching my heart. "You gave me a fright."

"That was an interesting lunch," he comments, ignoring my question.

I nod. "Yeah. So weird."

"A swarm of bats coming out of nowhere, attacking Felix like that. Very unusual."

"Very."

He raises his eyebrows. "You're not going to go outside and enjoy the spectacle? The bats are drawing quite a crowd. The whole school is out there. It's already up online."

He holds out his phone and shows me a video on YouTube of Felix being chased by the bats and screaming, "I THINK THERE'S ONE IN MY HAIR!"

I try to suppress a giggle. "Oh no, poor Felix. I'm not interested in watching but you go ahead."

"Nah, I'm not that interested either." He shrugs. "Hey, so do you remember when we first met? You were looking for old sorcery books, weren't you?"

I shake my head. "No, I don't think so. I can't remember."

"Well, I remembered that the other day, and I found one in the back of my dad's shop. It's absolutely hilarious. Strange what people used to believe."

"I can imagine."

"Have you heard of familiars?"

I freeze. "W-what?"

"Familiars," he repeats casually. "I was flicking through this book and it mentioned that people used to believe that witches had familiars to guide them. Basically, it was like having a sidekick in the form of an animal. A black cat, for example or" – he lifts his eyes to meet mine – "a tarantula."

I gulp. "N-no, I ... I've never heard of... I don't know what you're talking about."

He looks me right in the eye. "I think you have, Morgan. I think you know exactly what I'm talking about. What are you doing after school today?"

"I have a dance rehearsal for the talent show."

"I think you should cancel it and come to Blaze Books," he suggests, walking away from me. "We have a lot to talk about."

Chapter Eighteen

He knows.

No, he can't know. There's no way that he can know. How can he POSSIBLY know? He just can't.

Right?

"Can I tell you something?" Merlin says, sitting on my shoulder in the form of a dung beetle.

"Yes, please say something to comfort me right now," I reply urgently, swallowing the lump in my throat as I walk down the high street towards Blaze Books.

"All right. Here goes." He takes a deep breath. "You are sweating profusely. It's gross. My legs are actually sticking to you."

"Merlin!" I cry, touching my earphones so it looks

to passers-by as though I'm talking to someone on the phone and not out loud to myself. "We are potentially in a very bad situation right now!"

"Correction. *You* are in a very bad situation."

"He can't possibly know," I assure myself. "I'm just being paranoid, right? People don't go around assuming other people are witches. It's not what happens. Maybe his question about familiars was a complete coincidence and he ... he happened to ask me because I was the only one in the corridor. That sounds plausible, right?"

"Sure," Merlin says.

"There's no need to panic. No need to panic at all. It's coincidental that he happened to mention familiars to me, a real-life witch ... who happens to have a familiar. Right?"

"Absolutely."

"There's no chance he would suspect that a girl in his class at school is a witch. That would be crazy! Irrational and crazy. Just because I have a tarantula. Loads of people have tarantulas! Right?"

"Definitely."

"And weird things happen in schools all the time. Sure, a boy getting chased around by bats is a little out there, but there's no need to assume that Owen suspects a witch is behind it. Or do you think that because he's been reading that old sorcery book, he really is making the connection?"

"Uh-huh."

I hesitate. "You do?"

"What?" Merlin pauses. "I stopped listening a LONG time ago. What are we talking about?"

"You are the least helpful familiar EVER."

"Tell me something I don't know. Ooh, can we pop into this cafe and get a cookie?"

"No, we cannot pop into a cafe and get a cookie!" I practically yell, before collecting myself. "Merlin, this is serious. I'm freaking out! How are you thinking about COOKIES at a time like this?"

"It will be fine," he says in a tired voice as we turn down the empty alley towards Blaze Books. "Just pretend you don't know anything about anything. That shouldn't be too hard for you."

I push open the door of Blaze Books and try to act as normal as possible, and not like I'm sweating as though I've just run a marathon.

"Hey, Morgan." Owen is behind the counter with his dad, who gives me a cheery wave. "I wasn't sure if you were coming. I waited for you a while at the bus stop."

"Oh yeah, sorry, I had to stay behind for a bit to . . . uh . . . help with a thing."

A smile creeps across his lips. "A thing?"

"Yeah, it's nothing. Very boring. It's to do with ... um" – I glance at the row of spines on the bookshelf nearest me, looking for inspiration – "traditional Korean recipes."

Owen and his dad share a look.

OK, so it's not the best lie in the world but it's better than the truth, which is that I was hiding in the toilets trying to work out how I could get out of coming here, inventing various excuses that ranged from "I'm allergic to book dust so can never be in the shop's vicinity ever again" to "I think I'm dying and need to go home".

"Traditional Korean recipes," Owen repeats slowly.

"Yes. The school chef is thinking of experimenting with different cuisines and I was chatting it through with him," I say, as confidently as possible.

"You know about traditional Korean recipes?"

"I ... uh ... dabble." I clear my throat. "So, what was it you wanted to talk about?"

"Oh yeah, just some questions about the science project. Follow me." He smiles, nodding to the back of the shop. "We'll be in the sitting room, Dad."

We walk to the door at the back that, it turns out, leads into Owen's house and head into a nice cosy room with a wood-burner and shelves everywhere crammed with books. On the mantelpiece are photos of Owen and some holiday pictures with his parents. There's an unusual-looking antique mirror with a heavy, patterned gold frame in one corner of the room.

"Do you want a drink or anything?" he offers, gesturing for me to sit down on one of the sofas.

"No thanks, I can't stay long," I say pointedly, sitting down and clasping my hands on my lap as my fingers tingle with nerves. "So, what did you want to ask about the science project?"

He sits down next to me. "We don't have a science project. I wanted to talk to you about what happened at school today."

"What do you mean?"

"Felix being chased around the yard by bats. Remember that little incident?"

"Oh yeah." I nod. "That was funny. But I don't know why you want to talk to me about it? I don't really know much about bats."

"They're still following him. They waited outside the school all afternoon, watching him through the windows of the classrooms, and then when he left to go home, they chased him to his mum's car. He texted me a moment ago to say that they'd flown alongside the car all the way to his house and were now in the tree outside his bedroom window."

"Wow. They must really like him."

"Morgan, I know it was you."

"I'm sorry?"

"You summoned the bats to chase Felix because he was mean to you."

"What are you TALKING about?! How could I possibly have anything to do with bats?"

"I'm going to ask you a question, Morgan, and I want you to answer it truthfully."

"OK, shoot," I sigh.

"I'm just going to ask it."

"All right."

"It may sound mad. Completely mad."

"OK. . .?"

He takes a deep breath and looks me in the eye. "Are you . . . is there any possibility that you may be . . . a *witch*?"

There's a moment's silence as his words hang in the air. Then I throw my head back and burst out laughing. He frowns.

"Owen, WHAT is wrong with you? A witch? Seriously? Is this because you've been reading that stupid old book you mentioned earlier?" I shake my head at him, pretending to wipe tears of laughter from my eyes. "What do you think I'm doing in the evenings, sitting around a cauldron casting little spells over my friends at school? HA!"

"Not exactly," he replies calmly. "Warlocks use cauldrons. Witches can use spells at the click of their fingers."

I stare at him. My mouth feels dry.

"Anyway," I croak, "this has been an absolute HOOT. Seriously, you should be a comedian. Or maybe a writer, because your imagination is really quite something."

"Isn't it a bit suspicious that all these strange, dark things have started happening to Felix? The centipede on his arm – "

"It was a ladybird! He imagined it! Even he admits that."

" – the chair magically moving back of its own accord – "

I snort. "Sure. It magically moved back. He didn't just misjudge where it was."

" – wetting himself in front of the class – "

I hold up my hands. "Hey, no judgement here."

" – and as soon as he makes you look stupid, suddenly he's attacked by a swarm of bats, not to mention the random swarm of bats that happened to appear at a party where you were dressed as a vampire and then leave the party with you," he continues, standing up and pacing around his sitting room. "It all points to you being a witch!"

"Owen, you have lost your mind! Can you hear what you're saying?"

"Tell me about the dancing, then."

"What about the dancing?" I ask, checking my watch and trying to ignore the fact that my cheeks are growing hotter and hotter.

"Do you expect me to believe that you went from being completely uncoordinated to being a professional breakdancer in the space of a day?"

"Hey! I am not *completely* uncoordinated," I say defensively.

"Not any more. Not now you've clicked your fingers! Plus, there's your grades."

"What do my grades have to do with anything?" I pull at my shirt collar. It suddenly feels a little tight.

"You're suddenly top of the class. Miss Campbell remarked the other day that your latest history essay was university standard!"

"So?"

"You're thirteen!"

"I'm passionate about the Norman Conquest! I did a lot of extra reading and stuff. Look, Owen," I huff, "if this is to do with you being jealous of my recent achievements—"

"Trust me," he says, coming to sit down again. "I am

not jealous of any witches."

"You know more than one?" I snort.

"Actually, I do."

"*What?* This is getting ridiculous. Owen—"

"She's not a friend or anything. The opposite." He looks thoughtful for a moment. "I think she lives in Australia now. I met her when I was really young, on holiday in France. The only reason I remember her is because she had bright neon-green hair and she got in this huge fight with my mum. They had been friends as children, but they didn't know what each other actually *were* until they were teenagers. After that, they never spoke to or saw each other. Then we happened to bump into her on a beach in Nice." He shakes his head at the memory. "It was not a good day. She tried to put a hex on me and my mum."

I don't know what to say, so I just stare at him in silence, hardly daring to breathe.

"Morgan," he says quietly, "I know you're sworn to secrecy. But it's OK if you're a witch. It's OK if you have a familiar, who comes to school with you and guides you through life in various animal forms. You can tell me. I know about this stuff."

"H-how do you know about that stuff?" I croak.

"I'm not sure you want to know the answer to that question," he says, slumping back into the cushion, shutting his eyes.

"What do you mean?"

"Because you'll hate me."

"Why would I hate you for knowing about witches?" I ask nervously, before attempting a weak smile. "Are you a witch-hunter or something?"

"No. In your eyes, worse." He turns to look at me. "I'm a warlock."

Chapter Nineteen

The next morning, in history class, I can't stop staring at the back of Owen's head, thinking, *You're a warlock. A WARLOCK. An actual warlock. A WARLOCK*, on repeat. I'm so distracted, I don't care when Miss Campbell praises me for another excellent piece of homework. Even Merlin feels the need to transform into an annoying mosquito and fly right next to my ear to hum, "Quit staring at him with your big bug eyes! You look like you've gone mad!"

But I just wave him away and continue to stare at Owen's head some more.

HOW COULD THIS HAPPEN?

Do you know how rare it is to be a witch? And how rare it is to be a warlock? And how unlikely it is to end up at the SAME SCHOOL in the SAME CLASS together?! It's so mad, I can't get my head round it.

When Owen told me this little secret of his last night, I was so terrified, I fell off the sofa.

Like, actually fell right off the sofa and on to the ground.

Once I'd scrambled off the floor on to my feet, I backed away from him in fear.

"It's OK, I'm not going to hurt you. This isn't some kind of trap," he said, looking startled and then a bit hurt at my reaction. "You know me, Morgan."

But I didn't know him. I didn't know him at all. A WARLOCK?! My sworn enemy! Sitting right there!

I eventually sat down at the furthest point of the room from him, on the very edge of the arm of the sofa, preparing myself for an attack, my fingers ready to click. But he didn't do anything. He sat there in silence, watching me. When I eventually found my voice, all that came out was something along the lines of "harrungumph".

And even though that isn't a word and I wasn't making any sense at all, Owen simply nodded and said, "Yeah. I know," in this defeated voice. Then we heard footsteps coming towards the sitting room and Owen looked panicked, leaning in towards me.

"Morgan, you can't tell anyone. No one can know. Right? I keep your secret; you keep mine."

I nodded in my dazed state and then Owen's dad walked in, bright and cheery, offering to make us a cup of tea, completely oblivious to the fact that his son had just told me, an actual witch, that he was an actual warlock.

I tried to be as normal as possible, but my brain was so overwhelmed that everything sounded like a blur of white noise before Owen saved me by telling his dad that I was just leaving.

"See you at school tomorrow," he said, guiding me back through the bookshop. "We can talk more about the science project."

"Urrghun," I replied.

"Morgan," he said, stopping me on the pavement as I stepped outside, "you might not believe me, but I'm glad. To be in it together. The science project, I mean."

"Mmmm," I said and then walked towards the bus stop feeling as though I might throw up all over the pavement.

Merlin was as shocked as I was, but as I might have suspected, his reaction was a little different to mine. While I spent the evening lying on my bed like a zombie, uttering words that made no sense, Merlin darted about my room in various forms, concocting great magical plans.

I hadn't been listening to him at all, until something he said caught my attention.

" . . . and then we can destroy him once and for all!"

"Wait," I said, remembering how to speak. "What are you talking about?"

"I'm talking about how we ruin Owen's life," Merlin replied, hopping on the spot as a hyena and cackling gleefully.

"Why would we want to destroy his life?"

"Because he's a WARLOCK? You hate warlocks!"

"I know," I said, rubbing my head, which was thumping with all the confusion. "But he's . . . he's my friend."

Merlin leaped from the floor on to the bed, landing on my stomach as a baboon and purposefully winding me.

"Not any more, young witch," he said, scratching his head as I coughed and spluttered. "Warlocks are your great enemy, remember? Whether you like it or not, you can no longer be friends with Owen Blaze. It's the rule."

I never liked to admit that Merlin was right, but he had a point. His words kept me tossing and turning all night, unable to sleep as I struggled to comprehend everything. *How is it possible that Owen is a warlock? And if he is a warlock as he says, then what am I supposed to do? Are we meant to pretend that neither of us knows?*

Now, I'm just staring at his head, wondering how on EARTH he is able to copy notes into his notepad as though everything in life is just fine. I mean, look at him! He's just sitting there, writing! And putting his head up to listen to Miss Campbell! And now he's writing again!

WHAT IS WRONG WITH HIM?

"Morgan, are you OK?"

I start as Joe taps my arm, looking at me with a concerned expression.

"Are you OK?" he repeats in a whisper.

"Yeah. Course. Why?"

"It's just ... I've asked you a question about four times."

"Oh. Sorry." I clear my throat. "What was the question?"

"Can you teach me how to do a backflip? It would be so awesome to learn how to do that. You know, like, I could just be walking down the school corridor and then BAM" – he slaps his hand down on the table, making me jump – "suddenly I'm backflipping."

"Joe and Morgan, would you like to share your conversation with the class?" Miss Campbell asks, turning to give us both a stern look.

"I was asking Morgan to teach me how to do a backflip," Joe announces proudly.

"Ooh! I want to learn how to do a backflip!" someone calls from the front.

"Me too! Me too!"

Miss Campbell raps her knuckles on the desk as I slide down into my seat. She gets the class back in order, threatens Joe with detention and then continues with the lesson. I wait at least eight seconds before I return to my previous activity: staring at the back of Owen's head. He's a warlock. A warlock.

What am I going to do?

"Come and sit over here," Owen says at lunchtime, taking his tray to a table away from where our friends are sitting.

"But..." I glance at Iris and Lucy. "Won't it look weird that we're not sitting with them?"

"I don't care." He shrugs. "I have a lot of questions. Don't you?"

I have to admit that I do and so I follow him, trying to ignore the curious eyes of Iris and Lucy on us as we head to the other side of the canteen and sit on our own.

"Are you OK?" he asks, taking a sip of his drink. "You look a bit ... freaked out today. Every time I see you, your eyes are unusually wide."

"I am a little bit shocked," I say quietly, glancing around. "But I don't think we can talk about it here."

"Why not? There's no one listening. We can keep our voices down." He picks up his fork. "So, just to confirm, you are a witch, right? You didn't actually admit it."

I nod slowly, knowing that there's no point in denying it. "Yeah. I am. I can't believe this."

"Neither can I. It seems mad that we're at the same school. Like I told you, I've only met one witch before and it wasn't a pleasant experience. She tried to put a hex on me but luckily Mum had a potion stocked that cured it straight away."

"So, your mum is the warlock?"

"Yeah. Common misconception that warlocks are all male." He stops to grin at me. "Not that I need to tell you that."

"Right." I grip my water glass. "And your dad?"

"He has no idea. It can be difficult. I have to take my potion lessons in secret. He thinks that I'm enrolled in a cookery course some evenings."

"Yeah, my mum's friend is married to someone who has no idea she's a witch. She finds that quite tough sometimes."

He nods, watching me and keeping his voice so low it's barely audible. "Can I meet your familiar?"

I hesitate before answering, torn about what I should do. As a warlock, Owen is my ultimate nemesis and there is no way a self-respecting witch would ever introduce her familiar to a warlock. It's so personal, so trusting.

But this isn't just any warlock. It's Owen. And we're friends. He's the only person who's been kind to me at school.

"Yeah, OK," I say nervously. "Technically, you've already met Merlin anyway I guess."

"The tarantula." A smile creeps across his lips. "That has got to be the one thing about witches that I'm jealous of. You get a familiar."

"OK, well, let me just shatter that dream of yours right now. You would not want to be stuck with Merlin. He is the rudest, most unpleasant— OW!"

I clap my hand to my neck as Merlin nips me with his spider pincers.

"You all right?" Owen asks, confused.

"He just bit me," I explain, rolling my eyes. "What

was I saying? Oh yeah, Merlin's the worst. But you can meet him if you want. Maybe later when it's not so—"

Before I can finish, Merlin has crawled down my arm and on to the table. Owen notices the spider approaching him and glances up at me in excitement.

"Yep." I sigh. "There he is. Merlin, please behave yourself. We are in the canteen."

Merlin nods at me then turns back to face Owen.

"I might be making this up because he's so small I can't really see," Owen says, "but I think he's baring his fangs at me."

"Yeah, he probably is," I reply, stabbing at some pasta. "I did try to warn you. Also, he hates warlocks."

"Right." Owen wiggles his finger in an attempt to wave without anyone seeing. "Nice to meet you, Merlin." He hesitates. "He's now chomping his fangs in a threatening way."

"You've made your point, Merlin. Now, come back please before one of us squishes you."

Merlin reluctantly scuttles back across the table and on to my hand, ducking underneath my shirt cuff and crawling up my arm.

"I still think having a familiar is cool. What's it like learning to fly a broomstick?"

"Owen" – I put down my fork and lean in

closer – "firstly, I really don't think we should be talking about this kind of stuff at school where someone might overhear us. Secondly, we're meant to be. . ."

"Enemies?" He raises his eyebrows at me. "Do you think that we should hate each other now? Because I don't. I think the whole witches versus warlocks thing is stupid. The first time I met you, I suspected that you were a witch, but I didn't want to hate you just because of that. It seems backwards."

I'm shocked at the matter-of-fact way he's talking. How is he so decisive and calm about such a MASSIVE problem?! I've been brought up to think of warlocks as the worst kind of people, not to mention my experience of them being extremely unpleasant.

I shudder at the mere thought of Daisy Hornbuckle.

"But, Owen, it's just the way it is," I say, shifting in my seat. "Our history is so complicated. If Mum found out that I was friends with a warlock, she'd go nuts. She's the Great Sorceress."

Owen's eyes widen. "Your mum is the *Great Sorceress*? Whoa. That's intense."

"You're telling me."

"Does she know that we're friends?" he asks, biting his lip nervously.

"She doesn't know you're a warlock, so it doesn't

matter if she knows I'm friends with you or not. We'll just have to keep it that way."

"Morgan," he says, looking at me with a serious expression, "if your mum is the Great Sorceress, then chances are she knows I'm a warlock. She'll know everyone in the area who is a witch or a warlock. I'm surprised she let you go to this school knowing that a warlock attends it."

Now that I think about it, Owen is making a lot of sense. Mum would definitely know about the Blaze family being warlocks. I gasp as it dawns on me that that's why Dora is so against Blaze Books. It's probably nothing to do with the old witch books she doesn't want me to read. It's because the shop is owned by a *warlock family*.

"I guess Mum hoped that we'd never find out who each other were," I say, trying to make sense of everything. "There aren't many other schools in the area. I've always known I'd go to Riddle House. And maybe she thought she'd just keep an eye on my friends and if I mentioned to her that I was hanging out with someone called Blaze—"

"Then she'd forbid you to ever speak to me again." Owen sighs, and I guiltily look down at my hands in my lap. "Don't worry, my mum would be exactly the same.

According to her, witches are airheads who have spent thousands of years scheming to gain power but have yet to make any progress."

"Harsh. Well, according to my mum, warlocks are powerless wannabes who cause nothing but trouble when they attempt to make their little soups."

"Soups? Ouch!" Owen laughs awkwardly. "Those soups have saved countless lives. Not to mention the sort of power we can brew at the drop of a hat. Witches have no idea of what those *soups* are capable of."

I rest my hand casually on the table, as though I'm examining my nails. "A click of my fingers, Owen, and I can turn you into a toad."

"Or send a swarm of bats at me." He grins. "That reminds me, we need to talk about you stopping all that."

"Stopping what?"

He blinks at me like I'm stupid. "*Magic*. You have to stop."

"You can't tell me what to do. And why would I want to stop?"

"Because it's too dangerous, for a start. Are you even fully in control of your powers yet? I'm guessing you only just passed your YWE if this is your first time at school."

I tap my fingers on the table. "You are VERY close to being transformed into a toad right now."

"I'm not saying that to be mean, it's just as an observation." He glances around him anxiously. "Morgan, there are so many reasons why you shouldn't be using magic at school, let alone to the extent you are now. You could get a spell wrong and cause someone serious harm. And it's not like you're doing it very subtly."

"Oh please." I roll my eyes. "Like it's obvious that I'm a witch."

"I guessed it."

"You're a warlock!"

"Still, you have to stop. You're just going to get yourself into trouble."

"I don't see how. And anyway, it's none of your business."

"Hey, Morgan!"

Iris's voice makes us spring apart, jumping back in our seats from where we were leaning forwards across the table.

"This seems cosy," she says, with a knowing look. "Am I interrupting?"

"No! No, we were just . . . it's a . . . traditional Korean recipes thing," I say hurriedly.

Owen looks unimpressed at my answer but goes with it. "Yeah. Morgan is a real culinary genius when it comes to Korean cuisine. I've been asking her for some tips."

"Oh. OK. That's ... random," she says, looking confused. "Anyway, Morgan, I wanted to ask you whether you'd be able to teach me some dance moves tomorrow after school."

"Me? You want me to teach you? But you're so good already."

"Not like you are," she says enthusiastically. "I think that you could really help me to improve and I thought it might be fun to have a lesson with you. Maybe we could choreograph some moves to add into the talent show routine. So, what do you think? Would that be OK?"

I find myself nodding. "Yes. Yes, I can teach dance. Because I can dance. So that makes sense. No problem. A lesson sounds ... great."

"Thanks so much, Morgan." She smiles. "I'll see you guys later."

"Well," Owen says as she walks off, leaning back in his chair and looking at me smugly, "this should be interesting."

Chapter Twenty

Iris puts her hands on her hips. "I'm sorry, Morgan, I'm still not getting it. Can you explain it again with a little more detail?"

I glance at the clock on the wall. We've only been here for five minutes. FIVE MINUTES. And it's felt like a LIFETIME. This lesson is not going well. I have no idea how to explain what I'm doing because I have no idea *how* I'm doing it. I'm making it all up.

"I'm not sure I can make it any clearer," I say. "You just step forwards like this. . ."

"Yep, I've got the step forwards bit," Iris says determinedly, copying me.

"And then you – "

I spin on the spot with perfect balance before

launching into a smooth run of amazing dance steps. I finish, smiling encouragingly at her.

"See? Now, you try."

She takes a deep breath and then steps forward, spins nicely on the spot and almost loses her balance. She wobbles and stops, burying her head in her hands.

"Maybe I didn't explain it properly," I say hurriedly, feeling a pang of guilt at her disappointed expression. "So you step forwards and—"

"It's OK, Morgan," she says, walking over to the corner to pick up her bottle of water and take a swig. "Let's just forget about it. There's no point. I can't do it."

"What?" I walk over to stand in front of her. "Of course you can."

"I don't know." She sighs. "We've tried so many times already and I can't even do the first move."

"Iris, we have been here five minutes. It may feel like a long time, I know, but you can't just write this move off already." I hesitate. "I think it's my fault."

"No, it's not. You're brilliant. I'm just ... maybe I'm not good enough for this level."

"That's not true. I'm a really bad teacher. Seriously" – I smile apologetically – "if anything I'm making you worse."

She can't help but laugh. "I have an idea that might help both of us."

"I'm listening."

"Why don't I film you doing some dance moves using a slow-motion setting? That way I can slow it down and study it, and then work on it myself, without you having to teach me. What do you think?"

"I think that's a GREAT idea."

I hurry into a space and when she's ready, she films me doing an entire routine. She watches it back on her phone and grins, giving me the thumbs up.

"This is great, thanks, Morgan."

"No worries." I put on my jumper and pick up my bag, before noticing that she's not doing the same thing. "Aren't you going home?"

"No, I think I'll stay here a while and practise," she says, watching the video from the beginning. "I really want to crack one of these moves. Tomorrow, I'm going to show you that spinning step and I'm going to do it perfectly."

"OK." I nod, taken aback by her determination. "Good luck!"

"Thanks." She smiles, looking up from her phone. "Oh, and Morgan, before you go, I wanted to say that . . . well, I'm sorry for not being as welcoming to you as I should have been when you first came to this school. It's just . . . I really hate spiders."

"Most people do," I assure her. "It's fine."

"I mean it though. I shouldn't have let Felix make fun of you the way he did. He can be an idiot a lot of the time."

"Oh. Uh. Thanks."

"See you tomorrow!" she says, looking back down at her phone and examining the video closely.

As I push through the doors, I walk into Owen coming the other way.

"What are *you* doing here?"

"I was coming to watch the rehearsal," he explains, looking at his watch in confusion. "I thought you promised Iris you'd rehearse with her after school."

"You missed it. The lesson is over," I say, walking ahead.

"How is that possible? School finished under ten minutes ago."

"I'm an excellent teacher."

He gives me a look and I roll my eyes. "Fine! It didn't go very well."

"What a surprise." He smiles victoriously, shoving his hands in his pockets. "Do you think that's because you can't actually dance and it's all a big fat lie?"

"Shush!" I say, stopping and checking no one is around. "What is wrong with you? Do you want to get caught? For your information, we decided that it would be better for both of us if she filmed me doing the dance steps and then learned by watching it back in slow motion. She's still there rehearsing right now using the video, so HA, I *am* teaching her." I carry on walking but this time with my chin held high. "It's a new method of teaching. Actually, it was weird, I saw a new side to Iris just now. I always thought she was really confident and perfect, but when she couldn't get that dance move at first, she was so down on herself. We'll keep doing the lessons this way and soon she'll be just as good a dancer as me."

"Except the difference is, Iris will have worked hard to get there and her skills will all be real. You just click your fingers and get what you want."

I sigh. "You know, it was a lot more enjoyable when you weren't commentating on my magic all the time. I admit I felt a little guilty when Iris was going on about how good I am at dancing. But if I hadn't used magic, I'd still have no friends and be a huge weirdo."

"When did you have no friends? And you're still a huge weirdo."

"At least I'm not a warlock," I retort. "I'd rather be the school freak."

He stops suddenly, throwing his arm out to stop me, too. "What did you just say?"

"Nothing." I get my phone out to call Dora and ask her to pick me up now that my rehearsal has been cut short. "Admit you're a little jealous about the fact that I can magic myself into an amazing dancer and you can't."

"You think I can't magic myself into an amazing dancer?"

"Obviously not, you're not a witch. You guys just ... heal people with herbs and stuff."

"WHAT?" He stares at me. "Are you serious? That's all you think warlocks do?"

"You do something else?"

"All right, that's it, Morgan Charmley," he says, waggling his finger at me. "This weekend, you're coming to mine and I'm going to prove to you why warlocks are better than witches."

"No way! I can't come to a warlock house!" I frown at him. "If my mum or any witch ever found out..."

"Then you'd better make sure they don't," Owen says brazenly. "Or are you just scared that I'll prove warlocks really are better than witches?"

I narrow my eyes at him. "Fine. This Saturday, I'll be there."

*

I arrive at Blaze Books on Saturday already chuckling to myself. Owen's whole mission to prove himself is hilarious. Merlin thinks that we shouldn't be bothering to entertain his notion and keeps warning me about spending time with him.

"You shouldn't be friends with a warlock," he's said a hundred times, repulsed by it all. "It's not right. And if anyone finds out, we'll be in BIG trouble."

I hate to say so, but Merlin is right. The idea of Mum finding out that I'm hanging out with Owen when I know that he's a warlock actually makes me shudder.

But I like hanging out with Owen. He's the only one who was nice to me right from the start. I can't believe that warlocks are evil, now that I know him. And I know it sounds strange because he's a warlock, but I like the idea of having a friend to talk to about magical stuff. Merlin once made the point that I'd never truly fit in at school because part of who I am would always be hidden away, but now that's not true. I have someone who gets it.

And, in any case, he's promised me that his mum is out for the day, so our secret is safe.

"We need to go up to the attic," Owen tells me quietly, patting his pocket which clinks. "I've set up my cauldron there."

I snigger at the fact that he's speaking about his cauldron so seriously and he glares at me.

"You have no idea what we can do," he informs me, and when he turns around I roll my eyes at Merlin, who is at my feet as a black cat.

"Why do we have to go up to this creepy attic?" I ask, after reaching the top of the creaky stairs and almost banging my head on the roof.

"Just to be safe," he explains. "Dad is in the bookshop and Mum is out, but I figured if we set up the cauldron in the sitting room and either of them came in for some reason, it probably wouldn't play out so well considering Dad has no idea I'm a warlock and Mum thinks your kind should be burned at the stake." He gestures around the attic. "This seemed like a good plan."

"Yeah." I nod, sitting down cross-legged in front of the cauldron. "Fair enough."

"Oh, and this is for you," Owen says, passing me a small illustrated children's book.

I take it and read the title on the cover: *Classic Warlock Fairy Tales.*

"Are you serious?" I flick through the pages. "You want me to bother reading these?"

"Yes, I do. I thought it might be nice to see things from each other's point of view," he says, sitting down on the other side of the cauldron, facing me.

"Oh. Well, thanks, I guess."

I put the book away in my bag as Owen pulls a load of glass vials out from his pocket and lines them up neatly in front of the cauldron. I peer at them curiously. They're filled with brightly coloured liquid.

"If we had the time to do this properly, I'd be using raw ingredients," he explains, as he picks up a big leather book and starts flicking through it until he finds the page he wants. "But as we don't have that luxury, I'm using a few pre-made mixtures."

"Witches don't need time to cast spells," Merlin points out, walking towards Owen and swishing his tail. "And they don't need ingredients."

Owen raises his eyebrows at him. "Witches also make stupid snap decisions with their instant spells that can cause destruction. Destruction that warlocks usually end up fixing with their well-thought-out, intelligent solutions."

"In other words," Merlin says, licking his paw, "witches are fun and warlocks are boring."

"Is he always like this?" Owen asks, turning back to his book.

"He's actually in a good mood today," I tell him as Merlin jumps back to me and starts clawing at my leg as he stretches. "Try living with it twenty-four seven."

"OK, here you go." Owen runs his finger down the page. "We'll start with this one."

"What's that book?" I ask, peering over the cauldron to try to get a look.

"It's a potions book."

"Cool! Can I see?"

"No."

"Why not?"

"Because you're a witch."

I sigh. "Fine. What potion are you going to make, then?"

"One that turns me into an amazing dancer," he states, before selecting a couple of vials and examining them carefully.

He kneels in front of the cauldron and, taking a deep breath, he closes his eyes and pours the first one in, a bright lime-green liquid. He then pours the next one in, which is dark brown. Merlin transforms into a wasp and hovers above the cauldron to peer in, while I kneel and shuffle forwards, looking nervously over the edge of the cauldron.

The liquid is bubbling, as though it's boiling. I double check beneath the cauldron in case I'm being stupid. No, there's no fire.

"There's no fire."

Owen opens an eye. "Well observed."

"How is it bubbling?"

"Magic." He smiles. "I need you to be quiet for a moment, just while I focus."

He picks up another vial and closes his eyes, placing his hand over the cauldron. He starts muttering something, which makes no sense; he's whispering gibberish. Mesmerized, I watch as he adds in the last vial, a black sludge-like liquid. As soon as it drops in, the potion turns to a beautiful, rich gold.

He opens his eyes and looks relieved at the colour of the potion. "It worked. Are you ready to try some?"

"What's in it?" I ask, as the thick gold liquid swirls slowly around the cauldron. "What was in all those vials?"

"If I were you, I wouldn't ask." He pauses and then gives in to my intrigued expression. "There are quite a few things in here; for example, a lot of herbs and then things like fish bogeys, hoof clippings, elephant saliva and a pinch of salt. And lots of other stuff, but I don't think you could stomach the rest."

I stare at him. He stares back. He's not laughing.

"Is that a joke?" I ask slowly.

"I told you not to ask."

"Fish bogeys aren't a thing."

"Yeah, they are. But only warlocks know that because we're the best." He dips a ladle into the potion and lifts it up. "Ready to try some?"

"I can't try that stuff!"

"Why not? Are you scared?"

I narrow my eyes at him. "No! But I'm a witch. We're sworn enemies. How do I know you're not poisoning me in your attempt to rid the world of all its witches?"

"Fine, I'll go first. This potion makes you good at whatever you want to excel at. You just have to think about it and you'll be good at it."

"No way. I don't believe you. There's no chance that fish bogeys and a couple of toe clippings can have that power."

"*Hoof* clippings," he corrects. "And it's not only the ingredients; there's a magical spell, too. Not just anyone can make this thing by having the ingredients handy." He points his thumb at his chest. "Warlock, remember?"

"You drink it and you become good at anything." I wrinkle my nose at the liquid sloshing about in the ladle. "I guess there's only one way to find out if you're telling the truth."

"Guess so." He grins. "Only take a sip. I mean it, a tiny sip. This is very powerful and we need it to wear off within a few minutes, otherwise we'll get caught."

And then without a moment's hesitation, he lifts the ladle to his lips and takes a sip before handing it over to me. Pinching my nose, I quickly take a sip and then drop the ladle back into the cauldron.

The effects are instant. It's like warm, delicious honey sliding down my throat and I feel a rush of adrenaline as the blood in my veins starts tingling.

"Check this out." Owen grins, standing up and then jumping into the air and doing five backwards somersaults in a row. I gasp as he swivels through the air, landing perfectly.

"What was that you said about warlocks being unable to make anyone an amazing dancer? Here" – he walks over to the stack of boxes in the corner of the attic, which are filled with odd bits and bobs, and pulls out an old guitar with a broken string – "play this."

"I can't play guitar," I say, taking the instrument from him.

But my hands seem to know exactly what to do and suddenly I'm playing the guitar solo from Queen's "Bohemian Rhapsody". I stop and stare at the guitar in amazement, while Owen cracks up laughing at my expression.

"This is insane," I whisper, my fingers running up the strings of their own accord. "I can't believe it."

"It's cool, isn't it? And this is all from a tiny sip. Imagine how powerful a larger dose can be." He folds his arms. "So, what do you think of warlocks now? You still think we just heal people and stuff?"

"I'll admit you've improved *very* slightly in my opinion."

"I'll take that." He checks his watch and grins mischievously. "We have about a minute or two left before the potion wears off. How about a dance-off?"

I put the guitar down and get out my phone, scrolling through the dance playlist Iris created for me.

"A witch versus warlock dance showdown?" I press play on my favourite song and music fills the room. "Oh, you're on."

Chapter Twenty One

The following Thursday, Owen finds me at my locker searching for the books I need for my afternoon lessons.

"We need to talk," he says, quietly but firmly, glancing around to make sure no one is listening.

"OK, but can we talk later? I'm just about to meet Iris to go through some talent show costume ideas. As you know the show is next week, so we don't have long to—"

"No, we need to talk now," he interrupts, frowning at me. "I tried to talk to you yesterday but you've been avoiding me."

"What? Don't be stupid! I have *not* been avoiding you."

This is, of course, a lie. I have been avoiding Owen for most of the week.

But it's not like I had much of a choice. I thought that after all the fun we had with the warlock potion on Saturday, it would be really nice to have a magical ally at school. I'd also read that warlock fairy tale book in one go on Saturday evening and I really wanted to talk about it with him. Once I started reading it, I couldn't put it down. Obviously witches don't come across brilliantly in any of the stories, but still, the fairy tales were seriously weird and wonderful.

There was the tale of Old Warlock Wickery who created a magical potion to stop the evil spells of the Ice Witch, Frigusa. She turned anyone wandering through the mountains into icicles hanging from the entrance of her cave.

Another one was about the warlock, Taraswin, who warded off a witch named Giorsal from taking over his village by creating a potion that turned all the villagers into wolves just before she got there. Believing the village to be deserted, she moved on, never to return.

I was especially entranced by the story of Ailfryd, a young warlock who went on a great journey to defeat the evil and most powerful witch, Koribella, who was ruling over the land using fear, cursing anyone who opposed her and taking away their spirit so they wandered the world like zombies. Legend had it that she kept the spirit of her most precious conquest – the greatest living warlock of the time, Xanthus – in a jewel hanging round her neck. Ailfryd played on Koribella's quest for ultimate power and tricked her into drinking a potion that trapped her spirit in the jewel, releasing Xanthus and all the other spirits under her spell.

But Owen didn't want to talk about the book, even though I brought him one of my witch fairy tale books to read in return, nor did he care too much about being my magical ally. All he wanted to do was lecture me. First thing on Monday, he went on and on about how dangerous it was to use magic at school and that he thought Saturday proved to me that spells were only temporary, blah blah blah.

"It's not real, Morgan," he'd huffed, jabbing his finger at my homework which had *FULL MARKS! EXCELLENT WORK, MORGAN!* written in red pen across the top. "You have to stop now before it gets completely out of control. You're going to get caught out."

"No I'm not," I'd replied, swatting his hand away.

"It's not like this is a big deal. It's just some stupid homework."

"And what about the dancing?"

"Once the talent show is over, I won't need to be a good dancer any more so I won't need to use any magic for that. So, please calm down. Geez, are all warlocks this gloomy? No wonder we don't like you."

I thought he might back off after that, but the next day when I happened to score eighteen goals in a P.E. hockey game, he gave me all these dirty looks across the pitch. Afterwards he launched into another one of his boring, spoilsport, magic-is-dangerous rants.

So, he can't blame me for avoiding him at all costs.

"Look," he says in a serious tone, blocking my route as I try to escape down the corridor, "I don't care if you've been avoiding me or not. The point is, you have to help Felix."

"What does Felix have to do with anything?"

"You haven't noticed that he hasn't been in school all week?"

"I know. He's got the flu. So?" I jostle the books in my arms. "It's been much nicer without him here making everyone's life a misery."

"He hasn't got the flu. He called me yesterday morning to tell me the truth." Owen hesitates as a group walks past us in the corridor. "Come this way; we need somewhere private to talk about it."

"Iris will be waiting for me and we only have a few minutes left of lunch break."

"Morgan, you caused a mess and you have to fix it."

"Fine," I sigh, following him into an empty classroom and slumping into a chair as he closes the door behind us. "If you want a cure for whatever illness Felix has, can I remind you that you are a warlock, so stop being lazy and make the potion yourself. I really don't have the time—"

"Felix is not ill," he states, refusing to sit down and instead pacing about the classroom anxiously. "He can't leave the house."

"Why not?"

"Because of the bats."

"What are you talking about?"

"The bats you summoned to chase him. You remember that innocent little spell of yours?" he asks impatiently.

I can't help but smile at the memory of Felix running about frantically as bats zoomed after him.

"I think that was a very imaginative spell, thank you very much. And anyway, he deserved it."

"Does he deserve never to leave his house again?"

"He doesn't need to be so dramatic! It happened one time; he doesn't need to worry about going outside. I promise I won't send a swarm of bats to chase him around again."

"Yeah," Merlin sniggers, in the form of a scorpion scuttling down my arm to sit on my hand, "next time you can summon a swarm of locusts instead."

"I was actually thinking a swarm of wasps, but locusts are *much* better." I grin, winking at him.

Owen narrows his eyes at me. "You know, right now I'm not sure who is more evil – you or Merlin."

"Definitely Morgan," Merlin says, pointing his scorpion sting in my direction. "Once she gave a witch at one of her mum's parties a piece of soap and told her it was a vanilla macaroon."

"OK, that woman was being openly rude about Dora's outfit so she wasn't a very nice person," I point out defensively, "and I didn't think she'd take such a large bite."

"Felix isn't being dramatic," Owen continues, "the bats are still there. They're sitting in a tree outside his house and watching him through the window. Any time he's tried to take a step out the front door, they've attacked him. I'm not saying he *won't* leave the house. I'm saying he *can't*."

I stare at him. "Are you serious?"

He nods.

"But that spell should only have lasted a day," I say, shifting in my seat. "They should have disappeared by now."

"They haven't. You need to get rid of them. Today."

"All right. I didn't realize." I bite my lip, wondering how those bats have managed to stick around. My spell must have been more powerful than I thought. "After school, I'll go to his house and see what I can do."

"I'll come with you," Owen says.

The door to the classroom swings open and Mr Hopkins appears in the doorway. He makes quite an entrance, swaying his hips and clicking his fingers, flamboyantly lifting his arms above his head as he begins to twirl on the spot. Although his body is dancing, his face is tired and glum.

"Oh," he says, noticing us as he continues to dance, "I was looking for Miss Campbell. Have you seen her?"

"I think she must still be in the staff room," Owen says. "Are you ... all right?"

"Yes. Well, no. It doesn't matter."

"Still enjoying your salsa lessons, then?" I note, offering him a smile.

He looks as though he might burst into tears.

"I *hate* salsa. I hate it. I can't stop! I just can't stop. Ever since that assembly, where I just couldn't help but dance, I haven't stopped. I can't do anything. The doctor can't explain it. No one can. I've been cursed to dance the rest of my life without any respite! The only time I stop dancing is when I pass out with exhaustion. But other than that, every minute of the day..." He lets out a sob, as his feet continue to dance. "I'm sorry. I shouldn't get upset in front of you. It's just, I love my job. I always dreamed of being headmaster. I'm sad I'll have to leave it behind."

"What are you talking about? Are you ... resigning?" I ask.

"A respectable school can't have a salsa-dancing headmaster in charge! I shouldn't be saying anything. It hasn't been announced yet, please don't tell anyone," he croaks, before dancing back towards the door. "Have a good afternoon of lessons."

With that, he salsas out of the room, slamming the door behind him.

"Let me guess," Owen sighs, as I bury my head in my hands, "that spell was only meant to last a day, too?"

*

As soon as we arrive at Felix's house, I can see that he's telling the truth. Perched in a large tree on the front lawn, right outside what I assume is his bedroom window, is a huge swarm of bats. If I wasn't in so much trouble, I would have thought it was actually very pretty, all those lovely bats hanging upside down on the branches, cocooned in their wings.

The road is a quiet one but there are a few people standing nearby taking photos of the strange phenomenon. I overhear a woman on the phone desperately trying to persuade a news reporter that there really is a swarm of bats who have set up camp in a tree in the middle of a small Essex village.

"I sent you that photo! How can you still not believe me?" she's saying in exasperation. "What do you mean, it looks photoshopped? I can tell you hand on heart it most certainly is not. You bring your cameras and come down here and see for yourself! They've been here all week... How dare you?! I am not looking for fifteen minutes of fame! There really is *an enormous swarm of bats* right in front of me!"

I notice Owen shudder at the sight of the bats and I put my hands on my hips.

"You're afraid of bats?"

"Bats are creepy."

"You're a *warlock*!"

"Yeah, exactly. We deal with natural ingredients like herbs. It's you witches who are into all the weird, gross animals."

"You put fish bogeys into a potion and then DRANK IT."

"Can we focus on getting rid of the bats?" He gestures urgently at the tree. "You have to do something about this!"

"Fine, I'll try. I don't know if I'll be able to," I admit, swallowing the lump in my throat.

"You did it before, right? You got rid of them at the party."

"Yeah, but these ones have been hanging around for a while and they were only supposed to be here a day." I bite my lip. "I'm not sure it will be very easy to get rid of them if they're this determined to stay."

"You have to try."

I sigh and roll up my sleeves. I don't actually need to roll up my sleeves to click my fingers, but witches do it all the time in movies and I think it gives a little more flair to such a dramatic moment.

Making sure that no one is looking in our direction, I nervously take a deep breath, focusing on the bats and willing them to disappear.

239

Then I click my fingers.

At first nothing happens and Owen and I share a worried look, but then the bats suddenly spread their wings in perfect synchronization and launch off their perches, flying up into the sky and disappearing from view.

"Job done," I say, breathing a sigh of relief as Owen smiles, watching them go.

A news van pulls up behind us and a reporter holding a microphone gets out, followed by a camera crew. The woman on the phone is staring at the now-empty tree in horror, her jaw on the floor.

"Where is this swarm of bats then?" the reporter says, squinting at all the trees down the road. "I can't see any."

"I *swear*," the woman whispers, "they were just here and then they flew off! Right before you came."

The reporter lets out a long sigh and shakes his head before turning to the crew. "Back in the van, guys, it was a hoax like we thought."

"No! No!" the woman cries, pointing at the tree. "I'm not lying! I swear!"

The van drives off and the woman stomps back to her house across the road. Everyone else goes too, leaving just Owen and I on the quiet, peaceful street.

"See, Owen?" I say smugly, turning to go back to the bus stop. "There was absolutely no need to panic and you can—"

A fluttering noise in the distance makes me stop talking as I try to work out what it is. We both look up at the sky as the noise grows louder over our heads.

"What is that?" Owen asks, squinting up at what looks like some small black dots in the clouds.

I gulp as the black dots get bigger. Whatever they are, they're heading straight for us.

"Maybe . . . maybe I didn't get rid of the bats."

"Wait," Owen says, shaking his head, "I don't think those are bats. They look . . . bigger."

"Maybe it's just some random birds flying around," I say hopefully, "and it's coincidental that they're heading this way at this very moment."

We both stand there in silence, staring upwards, trying to work out what's going on. As they get closer and closer, we can make them out more clearly. At first I think they might be eagles, but they're too small. They have quite long pointy tails, and large bat-like wings. And they seem to be . . . scaly.

"Morgan, those aren't birds," Owen says, his eyes widening as the creatures loom into clear view,

descending upon us at rapid speed. "They look like. . .
Wait, it's not possible. Is it?"

"*Oh no.*" I turn to him in horror. "I turned the bats
into *dragons.*"

Chapter Twenty Two

"So I think there may have been a teeny-tiny glitch with my spell."

"YOU THINK?" Owen yells, crouching next to me behind a hedge. "There are DRAGONS IN ESSEX!"

"Let's not panic. All I need to do is reverse it."

"Do you know how to do that?"

Merlin, in the form of a monkey on my shoulder, bursts out laughing. "She only just passed her YWE! Reversing spells is notoriously difficult."

"Maybe reversing the spell isn't the answer anyway," I say quickly, scowling at Merlin. "That would just turn them into bats again."

"You need to get rid of them. Completely!" Owen instructs.

We both peer over the top of the hedge to look at the dragons. At least they're *mini* dragons. It's not like they're huge and scary. They've settled down into the tree and are snapping at each other on the branches, claiming their spaces. I see Felix's curtains twitch and wonder if he thinks he's now losing his mind. I have to get rid of the dragons quickly. A swarm of bats you might be able to put down to a strange phenomenon, but a load of dragons chilling out in a walnut tree?

I'm in big trouble.

Owen ducks down again and looks at me expectantly. "Do you think you can get rid of them? Maybe we need to ask your mum to come and help."

"WHAT? Are you insane? We can't ask my mum! She would kill me!"

"Then you have to deal with this, Morgan," he says. "And fast, before people start noticing that there are dragons on their road."

"OK, let me focus."

I take a deep breath and close my eyes, attempting to shut out all the panic I feel right now and keep my mind calm. All I have to do is click my fingers and the dragons will disappear.

I open my eyes to look one of the dragons right in the eye. The dragon spots me peering over the hedge and turns his head at an angle, so that he can stare right back at me with his flaming orange eye.

My hand shaking, I click my fingers.

Nothing happens. The dragon, tired of being stared at, opens his jaws and shoots out a stream of fire in my direction. I duck just in time and the top of the hedge gets singed.

"That went well."

"Shut up, Merlin!" I shake my head. "I can't do it! I'm not a good enough witch for this kind of thing. *What are we going to do?*"

In response, Owen could have said "told you so". He could have given me a lecture about how I never should have used magic in public as I'm not a fully qualified witch and something like this was bound to happen. He could have just left me there and gone home so that I'd have to deal with it alone, considering it was completely my fault.

But instead he just says, "It's OK, you can fix it. We just have to work out a different way."

"What do you mean, a different way?"

"Maybe we use a spell to buy us some time, until you work out how to get rid of them completely. Could you make them invisible or something? Or try turning them into another, less-vicious animal?"

"I could try turning them into kittens!" I say, brightening. "Everyone loves kittens. And cats go up trees all the time."

"Give it a go," Owen encourages.

I click my fingers. Nothing happens.

Merlin, still in his monkey form, reaches up to examine my hand. "Is this thing on?"

"There has to be something else we can do," Owen says, his forehead creased in concentration.

We sit in silence, thinking, and then an idea pops into my brain.

"A fence! It's an easy spell to make one appear and I could make it look as though Felix's family are having some work done to the tree. As long as Felix doesn't leave the house, the dragons should remain in those branches and they can stay hidden from everyone else. I can magic a fence, I know I can. I've done it before."

"I can't think of a better idea."

"Is anyone coming down the road?"

Owen looks left and right before shaking his head.

I click my fingers and a high fence suddenly appears, towering over the tree and blocking the view of the house from the road. The dragons barely notice it going up; they're much too interested in Felix's window.

I sit back down, resting my head against the hedge.

"That will have to do for now until I work out how to get rid of them. Then you may have to try to make a warlock potion that wipes the memories of Felix's family. I imagine they're going to be a bit ... confused. Whatever happens, we can NOT tell my mum."

Owen nods. After a while he says, "This may be a bit of a disaster, but there is one positive thing that's come out of it."

"What?"

"You cast a couple of spells that were meant to last a day and they've lasted much longer. You turned bats into living mythical creatures, and they're determined to stick around." He sighs before bringing his eyes up to meet mine. "I think it's clear that you are a very powerful witch, Morgan Charmley."

The next day after school, I return to Felix's house to try more spells, and then again on Saturday morning, but it's hopeless. Nothing I do gets rid of the dragons.

And it makes it much more annoying that the dragons seem to find my attempts to make them disappear *hilarious*.

They sit on their stupid branches, laughing at me, steam pouring from their nostrils, as I crouch behind the hedge clicking away. And when I crane my neck to see if they're still there, they take it in turns to try to burn my hair off with their stupid fire-breathing. You'd think they'd be a little more respectful of the person who CREATED them.

I've decided I don't like dragons.

I had hoped that I'd get a moment to sneak into Mum's office to flick through some of her sorcery books and see if there were some answers in there, but she's had such a long week at work that she is determined to spend all weekend having "quality time" with me. She also keeps making everything worse by repeating how proud she is of me settling in so well at school and how happy it makes her that I've found some lovely friends and am achieving so highly in my lessons.

She really could not be giving me more of a guilt trip.

As I climb on to my broomstick at midnight, she continues her praise.

"Dora and I can't wait for the talent show next week! I couldn't be prouder, Morgan. The last few weeks, you've seemed so much happier."

"Absolutely. You're doing so well at school," Dora gushes. "You must be working so hard, scoring all those fantastic grades in your homework. Aggie, did I tell you that when I picked her up yesterday, I met some of her lovely new friends! There was Irena ... "

"Iris," I correct.

" . . . and Lily . . . "

"Lucy."

" . . . Zara . . . "

"Zoey."

" . . . and Katherine!"

"Kareen."

"They all adore Morgan, I can tell," she continues dreamily. "They were completely enraptured by what she was saying when I arrived and then when I came over to let Morgan know I was there, they told me how amazing she was and that they were sure they were going to win the talent show thanks to her!"

"Oh, how wonderful!" Mum beams at me. "I had no idea you were so into dancing!"

I laugh nervously. "Neither did I."

Not sure I can take any more, I push off the ground and soar into the air, pleased to have a moment to myself in the silence of the night, looking out over the trees. I hover, waiting for the others to join me, unable to shake the horrible trapped feeling that comes with lying.

"Right," Mum calls out, flying up towards me, "today's lesson is Emergency Stops. Very simple but important. You need to concentrate, Morgan, I can tell you're a little distracted. Now, putting the brakes on straight away is jerking the handle of the broomstick upwards – the difficult bit is maintaining your balance and not falling off your broom as it jolts into a vertical position. You ready?"

Dora and Mum demonstrate the move, soaring past me and then stopping suddenly. I watch them and when they've gone through it, they ask if I'm ready to give it a go.

I zoom through the air, that feeling of guilt washing away as I get the adrenaline rush of flying through the trees. But then, just as Mum signals for me to practise the emergency stop, I hear a sound in the distance. It's a high-pitched screech that makes Dora and Mum share a confused look.

It's a dragon cry.

I'm so distracted by the cry that I forget to do my emergency stop and ... *THWACK!*

I fly straight into a tree, slipping from my broom and hurtling towards the ground. At the click of Mum's fingers, my fall is stopped and I float down gently until I'm sitting at the foot of the tree.

"Are you OK, Morgan?" Mum asks, as she and Dora land next to me and crouch down in concern.

Rubbing my bruised nose, I feel sick with worry about how to deal with those dragons. If they keep crying out like that, Mum and any other witches in the area might get suspicious, and if any of them find out that I've caused dragons to appear in full view of non-magic folk, as well as all the strange goings-on at my school...

I wouldn't be allowed back to school, maybe ever. They wouldn't risk me giving away the secret again. I'm finally enjoying school! I don't want to go back to being on my own all the time. Would they ban me from using magic in public for the rest of my life? Or worse, using magic *at all*? And what about Mum's position as the Great Sorceress? She might be asked to step down.

"I'm fine. Everything's fine."

But everything *isn't* fine. And it's about to get worse.

Chapter Twenty Three

"Morgan," Iris says slowly, stopping the music as the others stare at me in confused silence, "are you all right?"

Our rehearsal had just started and we were going through the dance from the top. As usual, I'd clicked my fingers during our warm-up stretches and taken my place front and centre. The music had started and I'd prepared myself for that familiar feeling of magic running through my veins and my feet just launching into the routine.

That didn't happen. Nothing happened. I just stood there.

And when I'd tried to do one of the steps, I'd tripped over my own feet, stumbled forwards and knocked into Iris.

"Sorry," I say, my cheeks growing hot with embarrassment. "I'm not sure what happened there."

"Shall we try again from the beginning?"

"Yes. Let's go. Sorry, I'll concentrate this time."

Iris smiles and then goes back to her place, picking up her phone to play the song from the start. Pretending to shake out my hands, I click my fingers.

Nothing. My feet won't do anything. My arms won't do anything. I try moving them to kick them into action, but it doesn't work and I'm standing there flailing my arms about as the rest of the group dance in perfect unison around me.

"Uh-oh," Merlin whispers, zipping about my head in the form of a fruit fly. "Something's wrong."

"Morgan, what's going on?" Lucy asks as Iris stops the music again.

"Nothing. I just . . . hang on a second."

I do one last test. Pretending to click a beat out, I click my fingers determinedly and then attempt a backflip, something I've been doing easily almost every day for the past few weeks. I jump up . . . and fall on to my back.

The girls come to stand over me in a circle and I look up at their startled expressions from the floor.

I clear my throat.

"Would you excuse me from this rehearsal? I'm not feeling well."

I scramble to my feet in a panic and go to grab my bag from the side of the room.

"Wait, Morgan, you can't miss rehearsal!" Kareen cries after me as I rush towards the door. "It's a few days until the show! We need you!"

"Iris knows my bit of routine, right, Iris? You take charge," I instruct, waving at them before getting out of there and running as fast as I can down the corridor.

"Merlin, what's happening?" I ask as he flies alongside me.

"I don't know."

"Can you only use the exact same spell a certain number of times?"

"I have no idea!"

"Does this often happen to witches?"

"Not a clue!"

Do you know anything?" I cry in exasperation.

"I know that you're a rubbish dancer." He lands on my shoulder and transforms into a spider as I hurry down the school steps and run towards the bus stop. "Where are we going?"

"We're going to someone who, unlike you, might be able to help."

"Good," Merlin says as I stick my hand out for an oncoming bus. "Because you need a LOT of help. And fast."

I barge into Owen's sitting room after being directed there by his dad, and find him sitting with Jenny and the rest of his talent show group, practising their magic tricks.

"Hey," he says in surprise as I burst breathlessly through the door, "what are you doing here?"

"Can ... we ... please ... talk," I wheeze, having run all the way from the bus stop. "*Now.*"

Looking taken aback by my urgency, he nods and puts down the pack of cards he's holding.

"Hey, Morgan, while you're here," Jenny begins shyly, "I've been meaning to ask you, would you mind taking me through some notes on *Much Ado About Nothing* during a lunchtime this week?"

"Huh?" I wipe the sweat off my forehead using my sleeve. "Much a-what?"

She laughs, thinking I'm joking.

Owen, who has now come to stand next to me, says through gritted teeth, "You know, the Shakespeare play we've been studying in English? You got top marks in the class on your recent study sheet."

"I've been finding some of the language quite difficult and you're so good at Shakespeare. I thought maybe we could have a little study group and you could give me some pointers. Only if you wanted to though," Jenny adds hurriedly, her eyes on the floor, embarrassed.

"Right, sure. That sounds great," I say, causing her expression to brighten. "Yay, Shakespeare study group. Fun."

Owen gives me a withering look and gestures for me to follow him through the hall into the kitchen, shutting the door to the sitting room behind him.

"What was I supposed to say, Owen?" I ask defensively, already annoyed before he's said anything. "If I'd told her no, she would have thought I didn't want to hang out with her or something. That would have been so mean and I like Jenny."

"Have you ever read *Much Ado About Nothing*?" he asks, folding his arms and leaning back on the kitchen counter.

"Has *anyone* ever read it?"

"Aside from countless people around the world, yes, most of our class have bothered to read the play we're studying, including Jenny."

"Owen, I have slightly bigger problems right now than arguing with you over *Much A Few Somethings*, or whatever it's called." I pause dramatically. "I can't dance."

"What are you talking about?" he asks tiredly.

"I. Can't. Dance. I was in a rehearsal just now for the talent show and no matter what I did, the spell wouldn't work. Nothing happened!"

His forehead crinkles. "Nothing?"

"*Nothing*. I was back to being ... well, me!" I throw my hands up in exasperation. "On my way over here, I did a tiny spell on the bus, just to make sure I hadn't suddenly stopped being a witch and it worked. I focused on the head of the girl who was sitting in front of me, clicked my fingers and turned her hair bright neon-green. It worked like a charm, no problems!"

"Did you turn her hair back to its normal colour before you got off the bus?"

"Can we focus on the matter at hand here please?!"

"Morgan! She might have been on her way to an important event! You turned her hair green, that's not OK!"

"I didn't have time! The bus was suddenly at my stop and I couldn't get my brain to think fast enough! She can dye it back. Anyway, the question you should be asking right now is, *why* wasn't I able to dance when I cast my spell just the same as I always do?"

He sighs, shaking his head, and I wait impatiently for his answer, tapping my nails on the side.

"You know the answer to that question," he says eventually.

"What? No I don't!"

"Yes, you do," he insists. "I've told you so many times. *Magic isn't real*. That's why it's magic!"

"That doesn't mean anything. If I do a spell, it should work."

"Should it? You think it's that easy? In that case, why didn't you pass your YWE at the age of five, the first time you took it?" He watches me carefully. "Magic is never simple. It's a supernatural power, but it's also a craft and it takes years to perfect. I'm sure even your mum still makes mistakes; I know my mum messes up potions sometimes. Why do you think the best witches and warlocks keep a low profile? They don't go around clicking their fingers and becoming famous musicians or athletes. It's impossible to keep up something that isn't real in the first place, not to mention how tiring it must be pretending to be someone you're not."

I let his words sink in. "So, that's it? The dance magic has all gone and I won't be able to get it back?"

He shrugs. "I don't know."

"I need you to make that potion. The one which

makes you good at everything. I can take it right before the talent show and then everything will be fine."

He looks at me as though I'm mad.

"No way! Haven't you listened to a word I've just said?"

"I know you can make that potion, Owen, I've seen you do it!"

"We used up a lot of those ingredients..."

"I'll help you find more! We can go out together and track the ingredients down. Unless... Can I just use magic to make the ingredients appear?"

"No," he says grumpily, "the ingredients have to be natural. And anyway, I haven't agreed to make the potion yet."

"Why not?"

"Because it's *cheating*! I warned you something like this might happen and you ignored me. Have you sorted out the dragon problem yet?"

"I'm still working on that."

"And what about Mr Hopkins? He's resigning because he can't stop dancing."

"That's also on my list."

"Morgan, I think you should stop worrying about the talent show and focus on what's important. You're messing with people's lives! It's not too late to bow out of the show and let Iris lead the dance routine. She's the one who deserves to be leading it; she's worked really hard all term to improve."

"*Or* you could just give me a few sips of potion and I won't ruin the entire group's routine! They'll hate me if I quit! I don't know why you're making this into such a big deal," I huff.

"Because it *is* a big deal. You've been lying to everyone."

"Why won't you help me?" I cry in frustration, before lowering my voice as I remember the others in the room down the hall. "I thought you were my friend! If I don't get some potion, I'm going to look like a complete idiot in front of everyone!"

"I am your friend! That's why I'm trying to help you by telling you the truth! You can't just keep using magic to get your way."

"Typical warlock," I mutter under my breath, the rage bubbling up inside me.

He narrows his eyes at me. "What did you just say?"

"I said *typical warlock*. You're jealous."

"Oh yeah, sure, I'm jealous," he says angrily, "I'm jealous of the person who can't even control her own spells!"

"This is why witches can't be friends with warlocks,"

I blurt out. "You're jealous because I'm better at magic than you and always will be!"

I regret the words as soon as I say them. Owen recoils as though someone's slapped him, his eyes full of hurt.

"You should go, Morgan," he says quietly, opening the door and heading back down the hall. "I'll see you at school."

"Owen," I croak, going after him, "wait, I didn't—"

He slams the sitting-room door behind him, leaving me standing on my own in the silence of the hallway.

Chapter Twenty Four

A steaming mug of hot chocolate floats through the room and hovers above my pillow.

I lift my head to see Mum leaning against my bedroom door.

"Can I come in?" she asks.

I slump back against my pillow where Merlin is curled up next to my head in his black cat form. "Sure."

She walks round my bed and budges my legs over so that she can sit on the edge. Helena, in the form of a swallow, flies in and lands neatly on her knee. Mum nods to the mug still floating above my head.

"I gave you extra marshmallows."

"Thanks."

"I thought you might want to talk," she says gently.

"Dora mentioned that you asked her to pick you up at the normal time today. Weren't you supposed to be staying late to do your dress rehearsal for the talent show tomorrow?"

"I didn't feel up to it."

She nods. "Is everything all right? You've seemed down this week."

"I'm OK."

She doesn't say anything and I continue to stare up at the ceiling, playing with my necklace in silence. After a long pause, as I realize that she isn't going to budge any time soon, I let out a sigh.

"Mum?"

"Yes?"

"Did you ever find it difficult to fit in without using magic?"

She takes her time to answer, thinking carefully. "Yes, and I still do even now. Hiding a part of who you are is never easy."

I hoist myself up and plump up my pillows to sit back against them, annoying Merlin who transforms into a bat and goes to hang off the curtain rail in peace. I pick up the mug of hot chocolate and take a sip.

It's been a weird few days.

Since I interrupted his magic-trick night, Owen has

barely spoken a word to me. I felt so bad about what I said and tried talking to him before lessons the next day, but he brushed me off.

When I tried to say sorry, he lifted his eyebrows at me all cynically and said, "Are you apologizing because you want to be friends again, or is it because you want me to give you that potion?"

"Don't be stupid. I'm saying sorry because I mean it. That's all."

"I never thought that you'd believe all that stupid witch versus warlock stuff," he replied quietly. "I thought you were cooler than that."

I tried talking to him again, but he wasn't interested in listening. I must have really hurt his feelings and I didn't know how to make it better. Felix's empty chair was putting me in an even worse mood – the dragon situation was always in the back of my mind. I needed to come up with a solution.

And then, as if all that wasn't enough to think about, there were the rumours about the headmaster. It was Joe who first mentioned it to me just before the start of our lesson with Miss Campbell yesterday morning.

"Did you hear all this stuff about Mr Hopkins?" he asked as I took my seat next to him.

"No?"

"Apparently, he's become this recluse and he won't come out of his house."

One of the boys at the desk in front of us had swivelled round in his seat to join the conversation. "I heard that he got arrested. My mum's friend saw him dancing with random people in the supermarket and someone filed a complaint. A police officer came to talk to him but he kept dancing around them, so they arrested him for refusing to cooperate."

"*What?* And now he won't leave his house?"

"That's right," Joe had confirmed solemnly. "I feel bad for him actually. He was a bit grumpy, but he wasn't that bad."

I felt terrible. Not only had I trapped Felix in his home, I'd also isolated Mr Hopkins. He and I had never exactly seen eye to eye, but I'd never meant for it to go this far.

I'd been completely distracted the rest of the day and was dreading the dance rehearsal. I decided to go, just to be sure the spell really wasn't working. Five minutes in, it was obvious that I was more useless at dancing than ever and I'd had to ask the rest of the group to practise the routine without me, saying I wasn't feeling very well.

"Maybe you have that flu that Felix has." Lucy had grimaced and stepped away from me.

"Do you think you'll be OK for the dress rehearsal tomorrow?" Iris had asked and I'd said that I would be.

Then today, I couldn't face it. What was the point in going? I had decided my time was much better spent going home and trawling through Mum's spell books just in case there was an alternative way of becoming a brilliant dancer again.

But the books in her office were much too complicated for me to get my head around. It was all really advanced magic. I put the books back and came to lie on my bed and stare at the ceiling, accepting the fact that the only way I could possibly be in the talent show would be for Owen to give me some of that potion.

And considering he hates me now, that wasn't very likely.

My phone is off so I don't have to see all the messages that the girls will be sending me, asking me where I am and why I'm missing the dress rehearsal the night before the competition. Tomorrow, everyone is expecting me to be the star of the show and instead I'll ruin the dance routine my group has spent all term working on. I'll be the least popular person on the planet.

The only thing worse than not having friends is having friends and then losing them.

I put down the mug of hot chocolate. "Sorry, Mum,

I'm not in a very good mood."

"That's allowed. Did you want to talk to me about anything in particular?"

I shake my head. "It's just ... I've made a few bad decisions recently."

Merlin sniggers, muttering, "That's an understatement," but we both ignore him.

"Well, we've all done that." Mum smiles. "Witches are notoriously good at bad decisions. Why else do you think we have such a bad reputation in fairy tales? We've been getting in trouble for centuries."

"Not you, though," I point out.

She tilts her head, looking confused. "What do you mean?"

"You got amazing grades at school, you were super popular. Now you're an awesome businesswoman. And that is all without magic. When it comes to being a witch, you're also the best at everything, and you just happen to be the Great Sorceress, the youngest ever to be voted into such an important position." I sigh. "I don't know how I'm your daughter. It took me ages to pass my YWE and now school is a complete disaster."

Mum listens to my speech and then she throws her head back and laughs.

I stare at her, insulted. "*Mum*, you're not supposed to

laugh at me. That was me opening up to you!"

"I'm sorry," she says, wiping a tear from her eye. "I'm not laughing at you, I swear. It's just so funny."

"What's funny?" I grumble. "That I'm a big failure in everything?"

"No, it's funny that you think I'm so successful at everything!"

"But you are," I say, frowning in confusion.

"Oh, Morgan, no I'm not. Did I ever tell you about the time at school that I tried to turn Melanie Cotton into a toad for laughing at my shoes?" She shakes her head, smiling in amusement at the memory. "I had these white trainers and I hated them, so I drew black cats and broomsticks all over them—"

"Like my backpack?"

"Similar, but I wasn't exactly a talented artist at the age of six. Trust me, my shoes were worse. Melanie Cotton pointed and laughed at them when I arrived at school, and then, because she did, everyone else pointed and laughed. I was so cross, I waited until I saw her on her own and when no one was looking, I clicked my fingers and tried turning her into a toad. Instead, I turned her into an umbrella stand. My mum was *FURIOUS*. Can you imagine how difficult that was to sort out? We had to get a LOT of warlock potion to wipe it from Melanie's memory."

"Wait a second." I hold my hands up. "You used magic in school?"

"I know, it was awful and I got in so much trouble. Why else do you think I warned you not to go down the same path?"

"She used it again when she was a teenager," Helena remarks. "That was even worse."

"You used magic at school more than once?"

"Look, please don't get any ideas," Mum warns. "I wouldn't be telling you this, but I don't want you thinking that I've never made any mistakes! I was thirteen and William Hedley made another one of his snide comments about me coming last in a race, as always—"

"Hang on. I thought you were good at sports!"

"Not at running. I was the WORST! I always came last. I may be good at flying, but I'm terrible at athletics. William Hedley was such a bully and I'd had enough. I snapped. So, I put a spell on him."

"What did you do?" I ask.

"Well, I meant to make him go bald."

"WHAT?"

"He had amazing, thick, glossy brown hair which was always combed perfectly, and I wanted him to know what it was like to not be so perfect." She rolls her eyes. "But it went slightly wrong. I did the spell in anger. As you know, that's never a good idea. Instead of just making his hair vanish, I made *everyone's* hair vanish. Everyone in the class, including the teacher. Again, a lot of warlock potion was needed to wipe those memories."

"Wow." I sit back, amazed. "I never knew any of this. Thanks, Mum."

"My horrific stories have made you feel better?"

"Yeah. I guess I don't feel so . . . alone."

She reaches over and squeezes my hand. "Morgan, you can be the worst at everything and I'll still be the proudest mother on the planet."

"Thanks, Mum. I wish I knew how to fix everything."

"You'll work out the right thing to do," she says, getting to her feet. "I'll leave you to your thinking. If you need me, I'll be in my office. Oh, before I go, this parcel was left on our doorstep for you."

She holds out a padded envelope with my name scrawled across it in untidy handwriting.

I wait until she's left the room and I hear her footsteps going down the stairs, then rip open the envelope. A small vial of golden potion falls out into my lap along with a note:

If you need it.

"Owen came through for you," Merlin comments, flying over to examine the contents of the parcel from my shoulder. "What an odd warlock he is."

"Merlin," I begin, staring at the vial of potion, "I've suddenly realized what I need to do. And I'm going to warn you now: you're not going to be happy about it."

"Why?"

"Because we're about to get grounded for a very long time."

I jump off the bed and run to the door.

"Wait," Merlin says, following me in a panic. "What are you—"

"MUM! Could you come back up here?" I shout down the stairs. "I need to tell you something after all..."

Chapter Twenty Five

"I'm telling you," the woman is yelling down the phone, "I know that I said bats last time, but they flew away. And now there are DRAGONS! You have got to send your TV crew down here again!"

Mum and Dora share a look. My fence may have kept most people in the dark about mythical creatures lurking on their road, but clearly it couldn't keep the most determined neighbours at bay. We watch as the woman throws her hands up in frustration, pacing up and down the pavement in front of Felix's house as we crouch behind the hedge nearby.

"I am NOT going crazy! Believe me, I've asked myself that very question many times! But I saw them flying down from the sky and then I came to inspect the tree after I noticed a fence had been built VERY quickly around it and I can promise you now, there are some kind of strange-looking animals up there BREATHING FIRE! I took photos on my phone! And before you suggest it, they are NOT photoshopped!"

Mum closes her eyes and shakes her head, while Dora grimaces.

"It could be worse," I say.

Mum turns to look down at me. "*How* could this be worse?"

"Um…" I pause to consider some options. "The dragons could have eaten someone?"

"That's true!" Dora nods enthusiastically. "They haven't eaten anyone. Yet."

"And they are quite cute dragons, as far as dragons go," I point out, nervously observing Mum's thunderous expression.

"Yes, very cute," Dora agrees. "I almost want to take one home with me."

One of the dragons coughs and a fireball hurtles past, narrowly missing Dora's head.

"Having said that," Dora squeaks, patting down her hair to make sure it's not on fire, "I'm not sure my spare room is big enough."

"I can't believe you didn't tell us about this

sooner, Morgan," Mum grumbles. "Do you know how embarrassing it is going to be for me to ask the Chief Warlock for enough potion to wipe everyone's memory of this? He'll laugh so hard and you know how much he spits when he talks? When he laughs, it's even worse."

"Not to mention you just gave him a long lecture last week about that warlock in Frinton," Dora points out, before explaining the story to me. "He was giving out potion disguised as tea at an old people's home. Next thing you know, there were grannies and grandads performing spectacular acrobatics whilst surfing! They looked like they were having a marvellous time. It was wonderful! But obviously very irresponsible," she adds when Mum shoots her a stern look.

"What is the Chief Warlock going to say when he finds out my daughter has turned Essex into a scene from *Game of Thrones*? He'll never let me live this down."

"The fence wasn't a bad idea though," Dora says, and I smile gratefully at her. "I'm sure a lot of people on this road have no idea what's been going on. Nifty bit of magic, Morgan."

"Yeah, well, I may be a terrible witch, but at least I can get the easy spells right," I say quietly.

Mum turns to give me a strange look. "What do you mean, a terrible witch?"

"Come on, Mum, look at what I've done," I say, gesturing to the dragons. "It took me years to pass my YWE compared to everyone else and I'm still messing up everything. I must be one of the worst witches in history."

Mum doesn't say anything for a moment, seeming deep in thought. Then she reaches forward and places her hands on my shoulders, looking right into my eyes.

"Morgan, this is your mess. You're going to clean it up."

"W-what?"

"You heard me. I'm not going to help you get rid of these dragons."

"But I can't! I've tried! I can't do it."

"Just like when you said you can't fly a broomstick? Or when you said you can't pass the YWE?" She folds her arms. "Funnily enough, those claims were both wrong and the same applies to this one."

"Mum, this is serious stuff!" I practically yell, wondering why on earth she's doing this to me. "I can't solve this one! I need a proper witch to do it!"

"You *are* a proper witch, Morgan Charmley," Mum says, while Dora nods along vigorously. "And the only reason you haven't been able to get rid of these dragons already is because you don't believe you can. As soon as you do, they will vanish at a click of your fingers."

"I don't think it's that simple," I argue.

"There's no harm in trying," Dora says confidently. "Come on, get up and go face those dragons like the witch you are."

"But—"

"You can do this," Mum says encouragingly. "Any witch that can summon this kind of magical creature is powerful enough to send them away."

I gulp and slowly stand up straight. A dragon spots me and tilts his head in amusement, delighted that I'm going to have another try. I glance at Mum and she's smiling at me in this knowing way. I take a deep breath and think about what they've just said.

It kind of makes sense. Any time I've tried to get rid of the dragons before, in the back of my mind I've been thinking that it was a lost cause. I knew that I couldn't do it, but I was trying anyway.

But Mum's words are striking a chord.

Any witch that can summon this kind of magical creature is powerful enough to send them away.

When I first created these dragons, Owen said he thought I was a really powerful witch. I didn't believe him.

But maybe I should believe him. Maybe he's right.

I stare back at the bemused dragon, who is now rallying himself to launch a fireball at me. I hold up my hand. These are not real dragons. They are magic. *My* magic.

I take a deep breath and I click my fingers.

For a moment, nothing happens and then suddenly, the dragons vanish. Mum and Dora jump to their feet and burst into applause, cheering as I look up at the empty tree in disbelief. Mum comes over to give me a hug while Dora dances on the spot, saying over and over again, "The pupil becomes the master! The pupil becomes the master!"

Glancing at the woman still yelling down the phone to the journalist, oblivious to anything going on behind her, Mum clicks her fingers and the fence disappears, while the brown patches of lawn, destroyed by rogue fireballs, are transformed back to their neat greenness.

"Thank you, you won't regret it," the woman says in a smug tone, turning round. "I'll see your team in a minute then."

Her phone clatters on the ground as she looks at the front of Felix's house. For a moment, she's so shocked, she doesn't speak but then she begins muttering to herself, her eyes wide with horror.

"B-but there was a . . . there was a fence . . . there . . .
the tree . . . dragons. . ."

"Oh dear," Dora whispers, watching the woman shut
and open her eyes again in disbelief. "We need to get her
some potion quickly. She'll think she's lost her mind!"

"I'll ask the Chief Warlock to get to her and Felix's
family as soon as possible," Mum says, heading back to
the car. "At least Felix is safe to leave his house now.
Well done, Morgan!"

As we get into the car and pull away from our
parking spot, the news van draws up behind us and I see
the camera crew hop out.

I slide down into my seat guiltily.

"Right, you have one more job to do," Mum says,
driving off down the road. "Where can we find the
headmaster?"

"Merlin and I followed him home one day after
school," I say, passing my phone to Dora so she can put
the postcode into the sat nav. "His house isn't far from
the school so we'll be there in a few minutes."

"What happened to the headmaster?" Dora asks.

"You'll see."

We didn't have time to explain to Dora what was
going on before we left the house. She had popped round
for a cup of tea as Howard was out at a poker night and

had found us getting ready to go, after I'd finished telling Mum the truth about what had really been going on at school this term.

Merlin isn't talking to me at the moment and has spent the remainder of the evening in the form of a flea, sulking in my jeans pocket. Mum has grounded me for the whole of the Christmas holidays and he's distraught at being shut inside the house for three weeks with only me for company.

Personally, I think we got off quite lightly.

When I started telling Mum about how one of my classmates was under house arrest due to some dragons that I'd set on him, and that I'd caused the headmaster to resign thanks to a dancing spell gone wrong, I watched her expression go from curious to shocked to very angry to very, very angry in quick succession. I thought that she'd ground me for the rest of my LIFE, so the Christmas holidays actually didn't seem too bad.

Anyway, I don't care what Merlin says. After a string of bad ones, I finally made a good decision. Telling Mum the truth felt like a huge weight lifted off my shoulders.

Obviously, now I actually know that I could have fixed all my mistakes without telling her, it does feel a little bit like it was all for nothing.

But, still. Honesty is the best policy blah blah blah.

When we get to Mr Hopkins' house, it takes a long time for him to open the door. Mum has to ring the bell five times before he answers and even then, he only opens the door a smidge so we can just see one eye peering at us.

"Hey Mr, Hopkins," I begin. "Sorry to bother you but, uh, we wanted to check that you were all right."

Standing behind me, Dora and Mum give him a cheery wave.

"Oh. Well. That's very nice of you."

"I heard you weren't doing so well and I think we might be able to help. Can we come in?"

"No, no, that's not a good idea," he replies hurriedly.

"It's OK, Mr Hopkins," Mum says, stepping forwards and giving him an encouraging smile. "I've heard of your condition before."

"Y-you have? But no doctor has ever seen—" He falters, unable to suppress a loud sob. "I can't stop salsa dancing! I can't stop no matter what I do! The doctors are baffled! They want me to be a case study! The first of its kind, they say."

Dora's expression brightens, turning to me in excitement.

"Permanently salsa dancing?" Dora asks, pursing her

lips to stop herself from laughing. "How on earth did you even get that idea?"

"Morgan, I owe you an apology," Mr Hopkins says, too distressed to have heard Dora's comment. "I was unfair on you at the beginning of term, resenting you for knowing the truth about my passion for salsa dancing which I'd hidden beneath my hard, intimidating headmaster exterior. Not that any of that matters now. I'm sad to leave my teaching career behind, but I simply can't carry on while I'm dancing everywhere I go. I imagine I'll need a hip replacement soon with all this swaying." He doesn't notice Dora's snigger. "Anyway, thank you for stopping by and good luck."

"Wait, Mr Hopkins. I told you that I've seen this before," Mum continues, putting her foot out to stop him closing the door. "And I know how to cure this. It's actually quite simple."

"It is?" He opens the door a touch more so we can see his face and hear the sound of his feet tapping on the floor. "How?"

"You need to have a sip of this," Dora says, holding out a bottle of water that we had in the car.

He takes the water from her and looks at it suspiciously. I realize that it's not particularly convincing. We could at least have taken the label off or something. Or cast a spell to change the appearance of the bottle.

"This is water," he says, taking a sniff.

"That's correct. But it's water collected from a mountain far, far, far away in an unheard-of, remote corner of the world," Dora says in her most mystical voice. "Very far away, right, Morgan?"

"Yes, that's right. A mountain named … uh … Big … Far Away … Mountain."

Mum rolls her eyes. Dora looks unimpressed. Mr Hopkins seems confused.

"Big Far Away Mountain?" he repeats, examining the bottle.

I'M SORRY BUT I WAS UNDER A LOT OF PRESSURE TO THINK OF A NAME QUICKLY.

"Not very originally named," I say, laughing nervously.

"It has rare healing properties," Mum whispers, glancing about her as though letting him in on a big secret. "Trust me, take a sip of that and see what happens."

"I suppose I might as well try," he sighs, lifting the bottle to his lips.

As he tips his head back, taking a good glug, Mum

nods to me and I click my fingers. He replaces the cap on the bottle and then suddenly his eyes widen. He looks down at his feet. He snaps his head back up, a wide grin spreading across his face. I breathe a sigh of relief. It worked. I did it.

"My feet! They ... they've stopped! They've stopped dancing!"

He throws open the door so we can see for ourselves, but I kind of wish he hadn't. Obviously not expecting visitors this evening, he is dressed in a pair of cotton pyjamas with teddy bears wearing red bow ties stitched all over them.

I will never be able to get that image of my headmaster out of my head.

"I'M CURED!" he yells joyfully, prancing forwards to give us all a big hug. "I'VE STOPPED DANCING! THANK YOU!"

Laughing at how happy he is, Mum insists that he can't tell anyone about the water from Big Far Away Mountain – it does not go unnoticed that she gives me a disgruntled look when she has to use that name – and says she looks forward to him announcing his return to the position of headmaster at the school tomorrow morning.

"Oh, I will," Mr Hopkins says, beaming at me. "I'll

see you in assembly, Morgan, and good luck in the talent show."

"Ah yes, it's tomorrow!" Dora says excitedly. "I can't wait. How are you feeling about it, Morgan?"

"I'm feeling good about it. Really good."

I catch Mum's eye and give her a smile, putting my hand in my coat pocket and wrapping my fingers tightly around the vial of potion from Owen.

"No. Way."

Lucy's jaw drops to the floor. Kareen gasps dramatically. Zoey looks as though she might faint. Iris doesn't say anything, folding her arms and watching me curiously.

"*What do you mean you can't dance?*" Lucy wails. "Get into your costume now! We're about to go on stage!"

"You're going to have to do the routine without me." I shrug. "Like I said, I can't dance."

"But we've seen you!" Kareen cries. "You're the best dancer ever!"

"We need you to win!" Zoey adds.

"No, you don't. Look" – I take a deep breath – "I haven't been honest with you, but I'm going to be honest now. You have all worked really hard to come up with this amazing dance routine. Iris, you can lead. You've done the routine without me for a few days now."

"I can't believe you're doing this," Lucy says, shaking her head at me. "I thought you were really cool, Morgan! But you're not, you're still just a loser!"

She stomps off towards the stage door that leads to the wings, Zoey and Kareen in tow. Iris waits until they've gone and turns back to me.

"Are you sure about this?" she asks.

"Yeah. I'm sorry to let you down at the last minute, but the truth is, you're better without me. You deserve to lead the group. And don't worry, I spent all night working on some cool lighting ideas and I went through it this morning with the drama technician dude. It's all ready to go. I spoke to Mrs Fernley and she says it still counts as a group project even if I'm not in the routine. So, you don't need to worry about being disqualified."

Iris nods, not sure what to say.

"Anyway, you better get on stage and I should be going to the lighting box. Good luck!"

"Morgan," she says quickly, stopping me as I turn to go. "Thanks. For the lighting thing. And sorry about Lucy's reaction and what she said about you being a loser. She's in a strop."

"It's OK, I deserved it. And anyway" – I shrug, smiling as I head towards the door – "if she says anything like that again, I can always sneak a friendly tarantula into her handbag."

Chapter Twenty Six

Mum makes me go to the party.

I didn't want to go to the stupid talent show after-party and it's not because I was *scared* like Mum accused me of being, it was because I needed time to study since I wasn't going to be using magic in my school work any more and that makes me WAY behind on every subject.

OK, fine, I was scared.

I have to admit that the teachers have managed to make the sports hall look much better than normal, with balloons and streamers and colourful decorations everywhere. Glitter balls are hanging from the ceiling, catching the lights, and considering it is Miss Campbell DJing, the music isn't actually that bad.

I hover in the corner for a bit, taking in everything,

and then wander along the side to the drinks table, taking a cup of pink lemonade and sipping it tentatively, wondering how long I have to stand here before I can call Mum and ask her to come and get me. I shouldn't have come.

No one in school is speaking to me.

The story of how I bowed out of our dance routine right at the last minute, leaving the most popular girls in our class in the lurch, spread through school in record time. I've had more dirty looks thrown at me than I can count and even now, hiding in the safety of the darkness by the drinks table manned by teachers, I can't escape the knowledge that I've doomed myself to being a social outcast.

"Did you hear about Morgan Charmley?" I overhear one teacher saying to another, unaware that I'm standing right behind them. "She quit. After all that showing off throughout the term!"

The other teacher tuts in disapproval and I tiptoe away from them, seeking out somewhere else to hide. I get out my phone and start drafting a message to Mum, informing her that coming here was a big mistake.

Distracted by my typing, I don't look where I'm going and bump into someone.

"Iris! Sorry!"

"Hey, Morgan!" She beams at me. "Sorry, I didn't see you, I was looking at the dance floor. I was hoping you'd come to the party. I wasn't sure if you would."

"Yeah, I'm going to leave actually. I'll see you later."

"Wait, why are you going?" She frowns in confusion. "It's only just started and we should be celebrating!"

"Oh, right." I offer her a weak smile. "Well done for winning the talent show. You really deserve it."

"*We* deserve it," she corrects. "It was a group effort. The lighting made it even better. Very cool disco vibe." She hesitates. "I'm sorry if anyone is giving you a hard time. I've tried telling everyone that it's not your fault. It's down to you that we won, you know."

"No, I didn't—"

"Morgan, you were the one who pushed me to be a better dancer," she says earnestly. "I was ready to give up, thinking it wasn't even worth trying to get to your level, but you didn't let me, remember? So, when I say that the win was a group effort, I mean it."

"Wow." I smile warmly at her. "Thanks, Iris."

Her eyes flicker to someone over my shoulder and her face lights up. I spin round to see who it is.

"FELIX!" she cries, rushing over to give him a hug. "You're back!"

"Hi, Iris," he says, laughing as she nearly knocks

him over. "I saw your routine; you were amazing! You deserved to win."

"Your group would have won if you'd been there to take part. Those yo-yo tricks were really quite something. How are you feeling?"

"Better thanks. I had the worst flu," he says, rubbing his forehead. "I can't remember much of the past couple of weeks, it's a total blur. It wiped me out."

"Wow, it must have been so bad!"

"It was going around, too. My whole family got it and, it turns out, some of our neighbours." He shoves his hands in his pockets. "Luckily, we're all feeling better now."

He notices me standing awkwardly behind Iris, pretending to be really interested in the wall.

"Weren't you supposed to be in Iris's dance group?" he asks, narrowing his eyes at me. "I heard you ducked out at the last minute."

"Oh, hi, Felix!" I say, as though just noticing him. "Glad you're back to normal."

"Morgan did the lighting for the routine," Iris says quickly. "I think it gave us the extra edge to win. That other dance group just had a white wash on stage and no colours or spotlights. Ours looked really professional."

Felix snorts. "You were so bad at dancing, they shoved you in the lighting box? That's hilarious."

My fingers itch to click together, but I clench my fist and force a smile.

"Enjoy the party," I say. "I'll see you both around."

As I turn and walk away I hear Felix mutter "freak" before Iris hits him on the arm and tells him to shut up. I smile to myself, feeling a little better about next term. At least I know that friendship isn't fake.

Now, I just need to save the last one I have left.

I spot Owen talking to Jenny and some others from his group and head towards him, shyly waving to get his attention. To my relief, he smiles when he sees me and, for some reason, I blush when I see him coming over to me.

"Hey," he says.

"Hey. Can we step outside for a second? I need to talk to you in private."

He nods and we head out of the hall, sitting down on the cold stone steps. Making sure there's no one around, I reach into my pocket and then hold out my palm to him, revealing the untouched vial of potion.

"You didn't need it in the end, then?"

"No, I didn't. I came to the conclusion that you were right. It wasn't too late to do the right thing." I sigh heavily. "Of course, it does mean that everyone hates me now."

He laughs, putting the vial away. "At least you have Merlin to guide you through this difficult time."

"Merlin's not speaking to me right now."

"Sounds peaceful."

"It really is."

The flea jumps out of my pocket and Merlin appears as a leopard before us. His bright yellow eyes narrow into slits as he turns to Owen. He bares his sharp teeth menacingly, drool dribbling from his jaw.

"He's a little angry that I followed your advice in the end and not his," I explain, as Merlin displays his huge, deadly claws by scratching them along the concrete. "He really wanted to see that new horror movie about the evil witches who take over the world with their zombie army, but we're grounded so I don't know if Mum will let us now."

"Sorry, Merlin," Owen says. "I can always go see it and then tell you how it ends."

Merlin growls, crouching into the position big cats take before pouncing on their prey.

"Hey, Merlin, take it down a notch," I instruct, checking around us again. "Any chance you can take the form of an animal a bit more local just in case anyone comes out here?"

He reluctantly transforms into a large cobra,

slithering up the steps and wrapping himself around my leg, lifting his head to glare at Owen.

"Great, that's much better," I mutter.

"I think you did the right thing," Owen says, ignoring Merlin.

"Me too. But thanks for getting me the potion anyway. That was really cool of you."

"No problem." He smiles mischievously. "I didn't want you thinking that warlocks were *total* spoilsports."

"I'm so sorry about what I said about warlocks, Owen," I say, seriously. "I was angry and said it without thinking. I didn't mean it."

"I know. It's OK. Honestly."

"If it makes you feel better, Mum made me speak to the Chief Warlock to ask for all the memory-wiping potion we needed for Felix's family and the rest of his road. He laughed in my face for a full ten minutes without stopping. There was so much spitting."

"That warlock has a lot of guts. I've heard the Great Sorceress is terrifying," Owen says, still chuckling. "What do you think she'd do if she found out that you were friends with a warlock?"

"I don't know. What would your mum do if she found out you were friends with a witch?"

Neither of us say anything as we ponder the question. I fiddle with my necklace. The air feels chillier, suddenly.

I have an idea of what my mum would do if she found out I was friends with a warlock. She would yell at me a lot, tell me I was never allowed to speak to or see Owen ever again, and then yell at me some more. She'd tell me I'd betrayed the entire witch community. I'd be grounded for ever. She would take me out of Riddle House and send me to another school.

I'd have broken the ultimate rule. Mum wouldn't be able to forgive me.

But just the *idea* of never seeing Owen again makes me feel sad. Really sad.

"No one magical can ever know that we're friends," Owen says in a quiet voice. "Ever."

"Right." I sigh heavily. "It's pretty risky, isn't it? Us being friends."

"Yeah, it is." He pauses and then says confidently, "I'm happy to take that risk though, if you are."

"Yeah. I am."

He turns to give me a small smile. I smile back. I suddenly find myself blushing again as our eyes meet. I quickly look back down at my feet before he notices.

"We should go in. It's getting cold," Owen says,

standing up. "So, are you going to keep practising magic at school next term?"

"Not if I can help it," I say firmly, getting to my feet, Merlin still coiled round my leg. "I want to stay out of trouble for a bit."

Owen tries and fails to suppress a smile.

"What?" I probe. "What's that look?"

"Nothing, it's just..." He hesitates, grinning. "You seem to attract trouble, that's all. Maybe it's to do with being a witch. You can't help it."

"Hey! Witches can stay out of trouble," I protest, a little more confidently than I feel. "I just had a couple of mishaps recently, that's all."

Owen holds up his hands, chuckling. "You don't have to justify it to me, Morgan. If I wasn't in control of my spells, I wouldn't want to risk using them at school either."

"I am *perfectly* in control of my spells, thank you very much! I'll just be putting them to better use next term. Like this."

I click my fingers and suddenly Owen finds himself wearing a clown costume complete with red nose and make-up.

"Very funny," he says, as I burst out laughing. "Is that the best you can do?"

I click my fingers again and he's dressed as an asparagus. Another click of my fingers and he's in a seventies disco outfit of gold sequins and sparkly purple platform boots. The following click, he's a big chicken.

"I'm going to get you back for this," he grumbles. I click my fingers again and he's suddenly Mr Potato Head. "Just you wait until I get to my cauldron..."

"Ooooh, your cauldron! I'm quivering in my boots! Just admit that witches are better than warlocks and I'll stop."

"Never."

"You've only brought this on yourself."

I shriek with laughter as he puts his hands on his hips dressed as a sparkly pink unicorn.

"You are the most annoying witch I've ever met," he says.

"I'm the *best* witch you've ever met."

When I click my fingers and he's in an aardvark costume, he can't help laughing along with me.

Suddenly, there's a loud gasp from behind us.

Spinning round, we see Iris watching us from the doorway, her eyes wide as saucers.

"Iris!" I gulp. "How long have you been standing there?"

"M-Morgan," she stammers, her eyes flickering to the cobra around my leg, "did . . . did you just say you were a . . . *witch*?"

As soon as she finishes the question, she promptly faints. I jump forwards to catch her before she hits the floor. Owen, still dressed as an aardvark, rushes over to help me lower her down safely to the ground. We straighten up and look at each other in panic.

Merlin transforms into a black cat, hopping up on to Iris's stomach as she lies unconscious on the floor and swishing his tail gleefully.

"Well, isn't next term going to be fun!" His bright eyes flash up at us. "What was that about staying out of trouble?"

Aknowledgements

Massive thanks to Lauren, Eishar, Aimee, Peter, Harriet, Kate and the ridiculously talented team at Scholastic. Your hard work made this possible and I feel so lucky to work alongside you. Thank you for believing in Morgan and bringing her story to life.

As ever, special thanks to my agent and genius friend, Lauren. You're an absolute inspiration. Thank you for saying, 'yes, that's a good idea', when I rang you and asked if I should write a story about a mischievous young witch and her sarcastic familiar.

To my wonderful family and friends, thank you for being my biggest fans. I couldn't do any of it without you. To my rescue dog, Bono, thank you for always being at my side.

And a huge thank you to my amazing readers. I'm so excited for you to meet Morgan and share in her adventures. Thank you for your invaluable support. You lot are, quite simply, magic (oh, and I know it's tempting, but try not to turn anyone into a toad. For now.)

Katy Birchall is the author of the side-splittingly funny *The It Girl: Superstar Geek*, *The It Girl: Team Awkward*, *The It Girl: Don't Tell the Bridesmaid* and the *Hotel Royale* series, *Secrets of a Teenage Heiress* and *Dramas of a Teenage Heiress*. She collaborated with Alesha Dixon on the bestselling *Lightning Girl* series. Katy also works as a freelance journalist and has written a non-fiction book, *How to be a Princess: Real-Life Fairy Tales for Modern Heroines*.

Katy won the 24/7 Theatre Festival Award for Most Promising New Comedy Writer with her very serious play about a ninja monkey at a dinner party.

When she isn't busy writing, she is reading biopics of Jane Austen, daydreaming about being an elf in *The Lord of the Rings*, or running across a park chasing her rescue dog, Bono, as he chases his arch nemesis: squirrels.